If the Sun Won't Come

KAYLA MARIE DUNLAP

WESTBOW
PRESS®
A DIVISION OF THOMAS NELSON
& ZONDERVAN

WestBow Press books may be ordered through booksellers or by contacting:

WestBow Press
A Division of Thomas Nelson & Zondervan
1663 Liberty Drive
Bloomington, IN 47403
www.westbowpress.com
844-714-3454

Author photo by: Anna Lovette, Trusting in Him Photography.
https://trustinginhimphotography.pixieset.com/

Scripture taken from the King James Version of the Bible.

ISBN: 978-1-6642-3880-0 (sc)
ISBN: 978-1-6642-3881-7 (hc)
ISBN: 978-1-6642-3894-7 (e)

Library of Congress Control Number: 2021913239

Print information available on the last page.

WestBow Press rev. date: 07/30/2021

To our soldiers and their families,
for their overwhelming sacrifices for freedom.
You will never be forgotten.

Contents

Acknowledgements

My deepest appreciation goes to my mom and my brother Mark for the dogged encouragement and honest critiques that have followed this book from its rocky beginnings as a short story to the final manuscript on the shelf. Mom, you have fostered my love for reading and writing from the first children's story you read me until now. Mark, creating stories and characters with you for the past twenty-some years has influenced my writing in incredible ways. I don't know what I would do without you two.

To my old friends Allura and Kayla ("Tater"), for inspiring my stories long before this story was even born. Allura, I still haven't forgotten sharing our book dreams and story ideas when we were teenagers; your encouragement when I was learning to write meant so much. Kayla, your dedication to the complexity and realness of your characters still inspires me to dig deeper into my own. Thank you, ladies.

Finally and especially, my praise and thanks goes to Jesus Christ, the Author of the world's greatest stories. Because of You, there is really such a thing as a happy ending. No story could ever be a beautiful as Yours, but this one's for You all the same.

Chapter 1

April 1945

The young soldier stumbled along, staring down at his filthy, travel-battered feet. Around him was Germany in the spring—cool but speckled with new grass growing in tufts and patches of flowers brazenly poking their heads out of the ruin of a war-ravaged countryside. Beauty could be found sprouting even here, if one looked for it.

The soldier was not looking. He was hungry. No, he was starving. He had never been this famished in his life. He felt like a scarecrow hobbling about, for he was nothing but a bundle of ill-fitting rags draped over sticks and straw.

He had experienced remarkably bad luck in the past few weeks. Yes, he had escaped the prison camp without being killed, and he had done it in late February instead of bitter December or January. Then, evading capture for weeks on end was a significant accomplishment. But he was not thinking of these blessings: he was thinking that his feet were raw and abraded from the terrain, that his throat was always dry, and that no decent meal for over a month had sucked the life out of him.

And then there was the sergeant.

The youth willed his aching legs and arms to go up a few more feet before he finally sank down at the top of a little

1

wooded hill. In front of him were more hills and more trees and more Germany. Belgium lay somewhere in the distance. Sighing miserably, he looked behind him for the sergeant.

Yes, just as he thought. The man was at least fifteen yards away, crawling through the grass with the speed of a snail. He was certainly never going to make it to Belgium. The soldier really had been a fool to bring him along like this, for all the man had done was slow him down and eat half the precious food scraps they found.

Eventually, the sergeant pushed himself to the foot of the hill.

"Come along, now, Sergeant," the youth said impatiently. "You're almost there."

Like a weary climber surveying the slopes of Mount Everest, the sergeant dragged his red eyes to the top of that hill. With an effort, he started to inch forward; but somehow he ended up on his back, staring up at budding green and blue and gasping for breath.

The youth decided this was it.

"Sergeant," he said, shuffling back down the slope, "what's the matter?"

The other man looked up at him but seemed unable to speak.

"Can't go on, mate?" the lad asked, bending down kindly.

The sergeant shook his head jerkily from side to side.

"It's all right, we'll rest a bit, mate," the soldier replied, grasping the man's shoulder reassuringly. "Then we can start again."

"Dear God," the sergeant gasped, closing his eyes, "I promised!"

"I tell you it's all right," the boy repeated.

Leaving the sergeant's side, he limped up the hill again and peered around. About a mile away, he could just descry the roof of a farmer's cottage nestled between a couple hills. Tiny wisps of smoke puffed out of the distant chimney and melted into the west wind. He thought he could smell cooked meat.

The youth looked back at the sergeant, lying there as good as dead. Jumping to his feet, the boy hurried down the slope once more.

"Good news!" he declared. "I see a house!"

"House?" the sergeant echoed slowly.

"Yes, and I'm going to try and filch a little food there," he said, reaching down and fumbling to undo some of the buttons on the sergeant's threadbare shirt. "You needn't come. I'll do it myself."

"What—are you—doing?" the sergeant murmured distantly.

"What I said," the soldier replied, grabbing the man's identification tags and yanking them over his head. "You just rest here a bit, mate, and I'll be back in a little while. We'll make it home yet."

Before the sergeant could respond, the youth blundered up the hill at a surprisingly fast pace. A moment later, the sound of his stumbling through the grass faded away.

Time passed. The sun crept toward the horizon. A woodpecker flew laughing into the trees. Still the boy did not return. And still the sergeant lay stretched out upon the ground, panting erratically and staring glass-eyed into the darkening trees.

⁓꙳

"Do you think we can build a sandcastle today, Daddy?" Eva asked, hopping up and down and tugging on his coat cuff. "You promised we'd build one soon!"

"I suppose we can," her father replied, smiling down at her sparkling brown eyes. "We've got to be home to Aunty in an hour, though."

"We can build one in an hour!" Eva squealed, dashing off to a short sandy strip that hugged a tranquil stretch of water.

Eagerly, the girl dug her hands into the grainy ground and began to pile clumps of sand into a fortress.

The place where they walked was a simple, ugly little shoreline on the coast of Southeast England. The gray sand Eva was excavating was strewn with sharp shale and seaweed—a beach not ideal for sunbathing. Most of the year, the water was too rough and dangerous for swimming. The rugged cliffs that marched above the ocean were more foreboding than picturesque. In fact, the whole area was much too commonplace and dismal for tourists accustomed to Brighton or the Suffolk Coast. Only the inhabitants of the old fishing village of Cot's Haven, a white cluster on the green-turfed cliffs overlooking the beach, cared much for their outlet to the sea.

But that was all right with six-year-old Eva Starbuck. According to her, she and her father did not need anyone else's company. Except her aunt Agnes and a few little friends in the village and at the girls' school, her father, Ulysses Starbuck, was her entire world. If the rocky beach was a little lonely, that only meant that there was more of it for the two of them to share.

"Come on, Daddy!" Eva called, swatting auburn curls out of her face. "Hurry and come make the moat. We don't have much time!"

Ulysses quickened his pace only slightly as he walked toward his daughter. The moment he was experiencing, watching Eva dance by the shore as her hair blew about her freckled face, was a bit of his life that he wanted to remember for a long time.

When at last he reached the construction site, he was just in time to keep the beginnings of her unstable castle from toppling over.

"Aha, you saved it!" Eva cried. "Now you can dig the moat!"

For the next half hour, the two labored to strengthen their fortress against all enemies. But as they worked, the growing wind forced the tide to advance upon the castle. Finally, a great roller rushed in without warning and leveled their work with one blow.

"Well, we enjoyed ourselves anyway," Ulysses chuckled as the water sank back to reveal a small heap where the castle had been.

"But the castle's gone," Eva complained, scooping up a handful of their creation and dropping it with a thud into the water. "Why didn't you save it again, Daddy?"

"I can't keep everything bad from happening, sweetheart," he shook his head, "even though I wish I could. But I can't keep the waves from coming in any more than I can make the sun come up in the morning."

As they strolled leisurely back down the beach to a little path leading up the chalky cliffs, Eva walked with her little left hand in her father's large right one, leaning her head against his arm.

"I don't like it when bad things happen, Daddy," she said.

"Well, neither do I," he replied, taken aback by his daughter's unusually thoughtful mood.

"And you can't stop all of them from happening, can you?"

"No, I can't. Why do you ask?"

"I was just wondering," the girl murmured, "what if the sun didn't come up one morning? What if it were always dark, forever and ever?"

"Sweetheart, you don't have to worry about that," Ulysses replied, bending down and kissing her. "I can't make the sun rise, but God brings it up every morning."

"Mightn't He forget to do it one day?"

"He can't forget, Eva."

"Oh, well," the girl smiled, "then I won't worry about it."

By the time they reached the top of the cliff and were hurrying up a little track to a row of tiny white houses near the edge, the sun had already disappeared over the horizon, leaving the sky only a vague glow of violet as a token of remembrance.

They had walked through their back garden and were approaching the kitchen door when the door suddenly flew open, and Eva's aunt rushed out. She was a short, thin woman with tightly curled black hair, sharp black eyes, and a bustling personality. Everything about her stood in stark contrast to Eva's father, who was tall and burly with orange hair, soft green eyes, and an unhurried demeanor. How they could be related was a mystery to Eva.

"Ulysses, where on earth were you?" the woman exploded.

"We were out for a walk, Agnes," Ulysses replied, startled. "I told you that."

"Well, yes, I remember," she said, whirling around and marching back inside.

"What's wrong with Aunty?" Eva whispered, having noticed the redness in her aunt's eyes.

"We'll see, darling," her father smiled, leading her through the back door into the flower-papered kitchen.

But they did not see what was wrong with Agnes—or at least, Eva did not. Dinner was unusually bland that evening, and Agnes was unusually silent during the meal. Twice she rose and left the room. The second time she returned, Eva was on the verge of asking her what the matter was, but a warning glance from her father shut her mouth.

"The post came, Ulysses," Agnes said abruptly, sitting back down.

"All right, Ag."

Agnes stared seriously at him for a second and made a curious noise in her throat.

"What's wrong?" Eva finally blurted.

"Nothing's wrong," her father said, looking hard at his sister.

"Nothing," Agnes restated, but her voice did not sound like she meant it.

Later that night, when Eva was crawling into bed, Ulysses poked his head through the doorway of her room.

"Hallo, Daddy! What is it?" she asked, fluffing her pillow.

"I've come to kiss you good night," he replied.

"But you already did."

Ulysses stood a moment rubbing his chin. His face was troubled.

"Well, would you like to do it again?" he asked at length.

"Not especially," Eva said, snuggling into her sheets. "I'm tired."

"Well, I'd like to do it again," Ulysses announced as he sat on the side of her bed.

Leaning over, he pushed a few curls from her face and kissed a rosy birth mark on her forehead. Eva thought he took a bit longer doing it than he usually did.

"My turn," he said.

Eva sat up, moved a tuft of his orange hair aside, and kissed a similar spot on his brow. But before she could flop back onto her pillow, her father grabbed her and held her tightly.

"I love you, Eva," he whispered into her ear.

"I love you, too," Eva yawned. "Please, can I go to sleep now?"

"Yes," he said, releasing her.

Eva smiled and tucked her coverlet up to her chin.

"G'night," she purred, closing her eyes as her father stood.

"Night, sweetheart."

For a few seconds, Ulysses stared at his daughter. Then he sighed heavily and turned off the light.

Chapter 2

When Eva awoke the next morning, her father was already gone.

"Where's Daddy got to?" Eva asked her aunt. "He doesn't leave until later."

"Don't ask questions, Eva," the lady snapped. "You ask too many of them."

Since her aunt was annoyed for some reason, Eva concluded that *she* was the reason and decided to make herself scarce that day. Hopping onto her bicycle, she rode into Cot's Haven to visit her eight-year-old friend Harold York. She found her dark-haired, dark-eyed playmate sitting in the little maple tree in his front garden.

"Hallo, Harold!" she called, dismounting her cycle and skipping over to him.

"Hallo," he muttered, peeling a piece of bark off a branch.

"Aren't you coming down?" Eva asked.

"No, I'll stay up here."

"Well, there's not room for both of us."

"So there isn't."

"Well, what am I supposed to do?" the girl pressed.

"Why don't you go play with that Amanda What's-its-field friend of yours?" Harold retorted.

"Butterfield," Eva corrected. "And Mandy's only fun if one feels very girly. I don't today."

"More's the pity."

"When are you coming down?"

"I'm not," he revealed.

"What do you mean?"

"What I say."

"Harold, did something happen?" Eva wondered.

"Don't you know already?" Harold returned. "My dad's been drafted."

Eva had been hearing that word a lot recently, but the only idea she had of it was that it was a bad thing that happened to men with good feet.

"Well, I'm sorry, Harold," she said. "But when are you coming down?"

"I'm not coming down until Dad comes home," Harold replied firmly.

"But that's hours away!" she protested.

"Hours!" Harold exclaimed. "Don't you know anything, Eva? My dad's been drafted. He may not come back for months!"

"Harold, what are you talking about?" the girl gasped.

"He's been sent to war to fight those rotten Germans. And if they don't kill him first, he won't come home for months or years, or maybe never!"

Harold slapped a few tears off his cheeks and turned his face away.

"Harold, that's awful!" Eva exclaimed.

"You won't know how awful until they draft *your* dad," Harold sniffed.

Eva took a step back.

"They won't draft my daddy!" she said, her cheeks flushing. "My daddy's not leaving me! He promised he wouldn't!"

"Well, so did mine!" Harold returned.

"My daddy doesn't lie!"

"Neither does mine!"

"Yes, he does!"

Still fuming, Eva leaped onto her cycle and pedaled furiously back home. When she reached her house, she saw her father's bicycle leaning against the front gate, but that did not strike her as unusual just then.

"Harold's daddy's a liar!" Eva shouted the moment she stepped into the house.

Her father and aunt were seated at the kitchen table and looked up in surprise.

"What are you talking about, Eva?" her aunt asked.

"He told Harold he'd never go away, but he's drafted himself, he has, and he's going to run away forever now," she declared hotly. "He's a rotten liar!"

Her aunt and father glanced at one another, and Ulysses looked as if he were going to be ill.

"Eva," he said, "Harold's daddy didn't lie."

"But he did!"

"Sometimes things happen that we can't help, sweetheart," he explained. "We don't mean to break promises, but they still get broken. Do you see?"

"Why are you saying *we?*" Eva questioned.

Her father took a deep breath and motioned Eva over to him.

"Eva," he swallowed, taking her hands, "I got drafted, too."

The child's face blanched.

"Remember I said I couldn't keep bad things from happening," Ulysses went on, squeezing her trembling hands. "But, sweetheart, I have to try to make them better when I can. I'm going to fight the bad things so they can't come and hurt you and Aunty."

"But you promised you'd always be there! You promised!" Eva choked. "And now you're going, and—and you may never come—"

A sudden hiccup strangled the rest of her words.

"I can't help it," her father said miserably.

"Yes, you can!" she cried, wrenching her hands from his grasp. "You can! You can! You lied!"

With those words, the child bolted out the kitchen door and ran down the path to the beach. When she reached the shore, she found an old drift log and sank down upon it in a pool of wretchedness. Dropping her little face into her hands, she broke into a stream of angry tears.

How could he do this to her? How could he break his promise?

"Eva."

"Go away!" she squeaked, not really wanting him to.

Her father bent down and pulled her hands away from her face.

"Look at me," he said as tears leaked out of his own eyes. "I've got to go. I can't help it. I can't make the war go away, but I can try to make it shorter. My little child, don't you see I'm doing this for you?"

"Why can't someone else go?" she whimpered.

"A lot of other daddies are going, too, Eva. I've got to go with them."

"But when will you come back?"

"I don't know yet, sweetheart," he said, hugging her, "but I'll come back as soon as I can."

Eva held on to her father as tightly as she could. Then she looked up and grabbed his face.

"What is it?" he asked.

"I don't want to forget you," she said, studying his features intently.

"You won't forget me, Eva," Ulysses assured her.

"Will you forget me, Daddy?" the child questioned. "Harold says you'll be away an awful long time."

"Eva," Ulysses said, gently rubbing the tears from her cheeks, "It doesn't matter how long I'm away. I will never forget you."

"Promise?" she whispered.

"I promise."

It was November 1939 when Ulysses left home. For the next six months, his daughter tried to adjust to his absence. Harold, after Eva had convinced him that he was doing his dad no good up in a tree, was some comfort to her. The two children spent many free hours together on the beach or in the village. But on days when their local cinema the Telescope showed the war newsreels, Eva positively refused to go with Harold and instead sought the company of Amanda Butterfield on her family's sheep farm. Playing shop or dress-up was a far better alternative to listening to Harold's personal version of the war news all day. She could not stand the thought of her father having to fight that evil man with the harsh voice and paintbrush moustache, and she certainly did not want reminded of the situation.

Letters arrived from Ulysses during those six months. While he wrote of how badly he missed Agnes and Eva, he would always find something bright and cheerful to say by the end of each letter.

You know, he wrote in one letter, *when I was in the Great War, I got a field promotion to sergeant. Maybe I can convince the Army to make me a general this time. Wouldn't that be first-rate?*

It was this lighthearted correspondence that helped to decrease the dread Eva felt about her father being drafted. She couldn't go and see him, but at least he was still safely in England

12

and not fighting anywhere foreign and dangerous. Perhaps having her father in the British Army wouldn't be so terrible after all.

Then May 1940 came, and the letters stopped.

"Why isn't Daddy writing us anymore?" Eva asked one morning when her aunt returned from the post office empty-handed.

"Your father's been sent to Europe, Eva," said Agnes. "We mustn't expect letters so often now. Why, it took six weeks for Harold and his mother to receive Mr. York's last letter. You've got to learn patience."

Eva did her very best to learn patience. She tried not to ask her aunt or the postman every day if the mail had brought a letter from her father with it. Later, she even got Harold to calculate the exact date that Ulysses' six weeks would be ended and then promised herself that she would say nothing more about letters until that date.

The day Harold figured happened to be the twentieth of June—a week before Eva's seventh birthday. And by the second week of June, Eva forgot all about being patient. Daily she waited in the bow window of the sitting room and scanned the road outside for the appearance of the postman. Although Agnes attempted to clarify that six weeks was merely an estimate and that her father's letter might come later, her explanations were useless to an excited child thinking entirely in absolutes.

The twentieth arrived.

When Eva came home that day, she sprinted to the bow window, parked herself on the seat cushion, and watched—and watched—and watched. The hours crawled by, each one an easygoing tortoise.

Then, around six, Eva spotted the postman cycling up the street.

"It's Mr. Bates, Aunty!" the child shrieked. "He's coming with the post! Daddy's letter is here! Come quick!"

"Eva, wait a moment!" Agnes called from the kitchen. "Remember what I told you about it coming later!"

But the girl had already flown out the front door and was sprinting down the walkway to the curb. She reached the street in front of the house just as the postman did. Her joy was so great that she felt dizzy with it.

"Hallo, Eva," Mr. Bates greeted, stepping off his cycle. "Is your aunty home?"

"Yes, she's just coming outside!" Eva pointed. "Oh, have you got it, Mr. Bates? Have you got the letter from my daddy?"

The man's expression contorted strangely at her question, and he looked up at her aunt. Agnes's face turned as white as her apron.

"May I come inside, Miss Starbuck?" he asked.

"Yes, of course," the lady answered.

Her voice sounded weak and small.

"May I have Daddy's letter first, Mr. Bates?" Eva pressed excitedly. "I can read most all of it, you know. I've gotten ever so good at reading. Aunty, I can read it first, can't I?"

"Eva, I'm going to talk to Mr. Bates awhile," Agnes returned. "Be a good girl and go to Harold's now. I will telephone his mother when you may come home."

"But Aunty, what about Daddy's letter?"

"Eva, please."

Reluctantly, the child turned and walked sluggishly to Harold's house. She found her friend on his front step, reading his own letter.

"Hallo, Eva!" he smiled cheerfully as she came closer. "And did you hear? After my dad was shot in the leg, it went so game that they said he'd be useless. And now they're sending him home!"

"That's lovely, Harold," she said, sitting down beside him and trying to sound happy for his sake.

"By the way, did you get that letter yet?"

"I don't know," the girl frowned. "The postman came, but he wanted to talk to Aunty, and they won't let me in, and I don't know what's the matter."

Harold let out a gasp.

"Oh, Eva, I'm—" he stammered, but he didn't finish.

"What is it, Harold?"

"Eva, I'm not sure I should say."

"Harold, please tell me!"

He said nothing, but the look on his face spoke for him.

Eva's eyes widened.

"I'm going now," she said abruptly.

When the child got home, she found the postman gone and her aunt sitting at the kitchen table, holding a small sheet of paper. A single tear was rolling down Agnes's cheek.

"What's wrong, Aunty?" the child demanded. "Did Daddy send a letter? Is he all right? What did it say?"

"Eva, sit down, dear," Agnes said, pushing her gently into a chair.

"What's wrong?"

"Your father's missing, Eva," her aunt whispered, struggling with her words. "The Army thinks he might have been captured by the Germans."

Eva stared at her.

"He's not coming home?" she inquired.

Agnes shook her head. With an affection she didn't often display, she brought the girl closer and wrapped her arms around her. The child swallowed hard but did not speak.

"He may still come home, darling," Agnes said softly.

"No, he won't," Eva murmured in a hollow voice. "He won't. He's never coming home. May I go now, Aunty?"

With numb legs and arms, Eva twisted herself away from her aunt and stepped clumsily out the door. If her aunt had called after her, she would not have heard it: she heard nothing and saw nothing. She simply found herself standing on the beach, without knowing how she got there.

Before her was the old drift log. As she sat down on it, she felt as dead as the object beneath her. Dimly she saw the gray waves coming in, felt the spray on her face; but it all was unreal.

And then Eva screamed. She screamed as loud as she could, until her voice was choked by sobs. But no one was around to say her name and console her this time. When the child was done crying, she was still as miserable and comfortless as before. And she had never felt so alone.

Chapter 3

That long, wretched war year came to an end. Then two more crept by, and with them went Eva's eighth and ninth birthdays. Although these were sullen occasions for her, the worst day of those years was Christmas. This day was her father's birthday, and the girl spent it wondering if he were even alive or if he were gradually freezing to death in a cold POW camp.

Another three years passed before May 7, 1945, when the Germans surrendered unconditionally. The next day, Cot's Haven, Great Britain, and the rest of the Allies were celebrating V-E Day. Four months later, the war, thank God, was finally over.

One by one, the soldiers of Cot's Haven came home—Mandy Butterfield's father, the postman's nephew Carter Tankard, Harold's cousin Walter. One by one they came home, but Eva's father did not.

Agnes and Harold's father Patrick York searched relentlessly for information about Ulysses Starbuck of the British Army, but no one would tell them anything. No matter how many letters they wrote or visits they made to various military offices, no one could help them.

"Thousands of soldiers are still missing," secretaries would say. "We are sorry for your loss, but the Army can't be expected to bring them all home. It's just not possible."

Still, they searched. But though POW camps were emptied, Ulysses was not reported among the prisoners that were released or buried, or in the records that were scoured. His tags were not brought back from any camp or any battlefield. Like so many other men, he had completely and utterly vanished.

Not knowing whether Ulysses were dead or alive was horrible for Eva. It was far worse than being certain he was dead, because then there could have been finality and closure. As it was, Eva was constantly being pulled back and forth between despair and a persistent hope that was almost as bad as the despair. She just wanted to stop hoping and go on.

But she could not.

In early October 1945, it was cold, wet, and dreary outside. A twelve-year-old Eva was sitting in her room studying when she heard the front door close. She didn't think to investigate. Someone was always dropping in these days to ask if they needed anything. It was probably Mr. York.

Ah, yes, there was his voice.

Eva turned the page of her notebook, trying to concentrate on algebra despite the voices that murmured through the woodwork.

Suddenly, there came a crash and a loud exclamation from the other side of the house. Throwing down her pencil, Eva rushed to the sitting room from which the commotion had come.

"What's the matter, Aunty?" she asked, hurrying to help her pick up the shards of a teapot.

Breathing rapidly, Agnes sank into a high-backed chair, still grasping a few pieces of the china in her hands.

"This is my niece Eva," she said feebly, motioning toward two men seated nearby. "Eva dear, this is Mr.—I'm sorry, I didn't hear your name."

"Short," said the thin, pale young man she had addressed. He flashed Eva a quick, almost guilty smile before looking down at his fidgeting hands.

"And this is Major Arnold," Agnes finished.

After nodding politely to Mr. Short, Eva turned her attention to the major. He was tall and gray-headed, with a smart gray moustache and an even smarter uniform with a crown twinkling on each lapel. While his face was stern, his eyes appeared to Eva to be rather kind. The girl started to smile at him, but suddenly the abnormal and alarming nature of a visit from the British Army struck her.

She felt the smile and color dissipating from her face. She wanted to say something, to ask if the major had come with news of her father, but she could not speak. She could hardly breathe.

Agnes sat in silence for a moment, trying to collect herself again. When she regained her composure, she turned to her niece.

"Eva, go do some of your revision," she said.

"I want to stay here," the girl pleaded, pushing the words out with difficulty.

"No," her aunt replied. "I'm sorry."

Slowly, stiffly, like some wooden wind-up soldier needing wound again, Eva walked out of the room, closing the door behind her. Her feet clumped down the hall and soon left her standing in her bedroom, with her heart slamming against her ribcage and her stomach churning.

Eva breathed deeply for a minute, trying to calm herself down. But she could not relax. The more she stood there, the more her mind raced and the more nauseated she felt. She couldn't stand the thought of sitting around in her room waiting for news that was being told right then.

At length, the agitation grew unbearable, and Eva decided to do something she had never done in her life. Swiftly, she wriggled out of her shoes and tiptoed into the hallway. The wooden floor usually creaked, but so lightly and carefully did she tread upon it now that it hardly made a sound. In half a minute, the girl was crouched outside the sitting room door, pressing her ear against the cold wood.

"I want the story plainly," her aunt's determined voice stated from the next room. "Don't try to spare my nerves. I am a very sensible woman, and you will not have to worry about me fainting or becoming hysterical."

"I believe you, Miss Starbuck," came the major's voice (a voice Eva had previously mistaken for Mr. York's). "Are you ready?"

"Yes, I am," Agnes returned at once. "He's dead, isn't he?"

There was a brief pause, but it was a sickeningly long wait to the child in the hall.

"Yes," the major sighed, "yes, Miss Starbuck, I'm afraid he is. Short here was the last man to see him alive."

"And I suppose Mr. Short has come to tell me how and where my brother died?"

"That is correct."

"I don't understand," Agnes continued, her voice straining under the emotion compressed inside her perfectly composed frame. "When my brother first went missing, all we received was a telegram. I still have it. I can tell you right now what it read. 'Regret to inform you that your brother reported missing in action. Presumed captured, possibly killed.' That's what it said. The Army didn't even bother to send a letter explaining what happened. Now that you know he's dead, what do you think makes this family worthy of a special visit? Why didn't you send another fifteen-word telegram? That would have been so much easier, wouldn't it?"

"Miss Starbuck, your questions are warranted," Arnold

replied. "I wish I could answer them fully, but I cannot. We knew your brother was captured, but it wasn't until much later that we discovered what prison camp he was held in. While I cannot elaborate more at this time, I will say that certain individuals involved with that stalag have given us reason to explore the case of every man in that camp with increased thoroughness."

"I see," said Agnes. "How fortunate we are then that my brother was imprisoned there, or I might never have learned the details of his death. And speaking of those details, please go on, Mr. Short, and tell me about them. I have waited a long time for this, and I would rather not wait any longer."

Eva knew she should get up and leave that doorway. While her aunt may have been given a strong constitution, Eva was already dazed from hearing that her father truly, officially was dead. But as badly as she wanted to go, she felt so weak that she could no more stand and walk away than sail to the moon.

"Well, mum," Short began with a trembling voice, "Sergeant Starbuck and I were in the same POW camp. Das Grab it was called, and it wasn't like any other. The Red Cross never came there, because the Red Cross didn't know it was there. I'm told the British Army only found it later by accident.

"Well, I was captured about a year before the war ended, but the Sergeant had been there long before me. When I got there, he took me under his wing, and mum, I never saw a kinder, braver man in the British Army than your brother. I can't count how many cold nights he spent without a blanket or pair of shoes because he'd given another man his own. I couldn't tell you how many of those meager meals he didn't eat because he'd slipped his food to another man, or how many times he took the beatings, mum, that someone else ought to have been given instead.

"In February of '45, I was able to think of an escape plan that really might work. At first, I didn't want to ask the sergeant to come along, because he'd already failed dozens of times to break out of that place. He'd kept at it, even when they started cutting off—well, I'll say the sergeant had tried to escape so much that the next time could have been his last.

"Anyway, I eventually decided to take him with me. I really did love him, mum. Why, he was like a father to me! That's why I asked him to go. You've got to believe that. I'd have never suggested he come with me if I didn't know my plan was sure."

"I believe you," Agnes said hardly above a whisper.

"We escaped," Short continued, "without a problem. It was glorious! None of the guards even knew we were missing, and they probably didn't find out until the next roll call. But getting out of Das Grab was one thing; getting out of Germany was another.

"I'm sure you heard the stories of all the underground groups in German territory, but they weren't so easy to find as the newspapers and magazines may have said. I swear we never found anyone to help us, not once. We were always hiding, always nearly getting captured, always on the move, always trying to steal a little food, and always, *always* hungry. You can't imagine how awful it is to really be famished, to be starving!

"It went this way for weeks on end. By April, we were both sick, far past starved, and only on the edge of Germany. But we still had Belgium to pass through, and, for all we knew, she was still held mostly by the enemy. You've got to understand, Das Grab was a world of its own: all the news we had was that the Nazis were winning everywhere. It was bad luck all the way with us, I'm afraid, for if we'd only been less cautious, we might have run into Allied troops marching through and both been saved.

"I can't tell you what day it was when we came to a patch of trees near a small farm in the country. All I remember is that it was raining hard, and the sergeant was completely spent. I was hardly better. We crawled under a big fir tree, and your brother just fell over onto his back. I could see every one of his ribs through his shirt.

"'You rest a bit, mate,' I told him, 'and I'll try my luck at that farmer's cot.' You see, we had to risk being reported or captured now, or we'd die. He looked up at me for a second, but I knew he didn't really know I was there. He was panting slow, like a dying dog.

"Well, I was able to pinch a bit of bread from the cot, so I came back as quick as I could. But when I got there, I saw the food wasn't going to be much use for the sergeant. He couldn't eat when he could barely breathe. His breathing just got worse and worse, until he sort of drifted off. I did think he might wake up again, but he didn't. Not five minutes later, he stopped breathing. I can swear he was dead, mum: I felt for breath or heartbeat several times, and I shook him and called his name. But he was gone.

"I took his tags, because I was afraid the Germans would find him and throw them away. There were rumors that some of those scoundrels did that. Here they are."

There came a tinkling sound, and then a brief silence.

"I'm sorry so many months passed before we could get this information to you, Miss Starbuck," said the major at last. "Private Short wandered long before a Belgian found him and got him to a hospital. And information is still coming slow and disorganized since the war ended. We also tried to recover your brother's body. That I'm sorry to say we were unable to do. It seems—"

Eva did not hear the rest. She did not want to; she could not. She hated that she had heard so much already.

To try to explain in words the intensity of grief she felt

would be useless. Her father was her life. He meant everything to her—everything. And now to hear that he was dead, that he had suffered indescribably in his last years, and that his body was now lying abandoned in rags under some dark fir tree in Europe, was utterly devastating.

Flinging aside all desire for stealth, she leaped to her feet, staggered a second, and then bolted down the hall to her bedroom. Once she had slammed the door behind her, she collapsed onto the rug and broke into uncontrollable sobs.

She had not been weeping long before she heard the door open and her aunt's high heels clack into the room.

"I'm—I'm—I'm sorry!" Eva cried into her hands.

Her aunt came and bent down beside her. For a moment, she touched the girl's shoulder with a clammy hand. Then she pushed something cold and hard into the child's palm.

"He'd want you to have these."

Eva's aunt stood and left the room, closing the door softly behind her. Agnes Starbuck was going away to be by herself. That was how she chose to grieve. But to Eva, being alone in her anguish was the last thing she wanted. Clutching her father's identification tags to her chest, she curled into a ball and wept until long after dark.

It was a warm day for October—warm, sunny, and almost hot. The leaves were still green. The grass was still lush under a deep blue heaven speckled with lazy white fleeces of clouds. It did not seem like the sort of day to wear black. But Eva was wearing black. One always wore black on occasions like this.

"Today we gather," came the voice, hollow and cold on such a day, "to lay a dear friend, father, and brother to rest."

Eva glanced up at the speaker, at his dark coat and pale,

solemn face. About him was a spray of black mourning and military brown. What was he saying? Her father wasn't being laid to rest. Her father wasn't even in the coffin.

"Though war has claimed another one of our good men in Cot's Haven," the speaker went on, "it cannot claim the memories we have of him, and the lives he changed while he was here."

Eva's gaze traveled across the open grave, over the empty casket draped in the Union Jack, through the crowd of flowers, to Harold standing on the other side of the coffin. He stood next to his parents, his face drawn painfully tight.

"Everyone who knew Ulysses Starbuck could attest—"

Gradually the words of the speaker faded out of Eva's consciousness. His speech sounded empty, cliché, and unworthy of her father. As she stood there feeling her feet ache in her tight new shoes, feeling the sweat beads trickle down her back, feeling her heart bang unevenly within her, all she could think of was what a perfect nightmare this would make.

Soon the soldiers would fire their rifles, and she would wake up. The kettle would be whistling in the kitchen. Her father would stumble into her room only halfway awake, buttoning his Sunday shirt and asking her where his tie had got to. Then Agnes would rush into the room bedecked in her floppy garden hat, throw the lost tie about her brother's neck, and grace her relatives with a brief discourse on the frivolity of sitting in a stuffy church when gardening was the only sensible thing for a fine Sunday morning.

"Ulysses," she would say, "you and that girl will be as pale as death if you keep this up. Why, what if—"

THOOM!

Eva flinched and looked round. The men were firing their weapons now.

"Ready!"

Cla-click.

"Aim. Fire!"

Thoom!

"Ready!"

Cla-click.

"Aim. Fire!"

Thoom!

She was still standing by the grave, her feet screaming, her back dripping, her heart hammering. There was no awakening. She knew there would not be. This was not a bad dream. No, she had been daydreaming about a nightmare, and this was the reality.

At last, the funeral ended, and the ladies went back to their house. It was just a house now, not home. When Eva stepped inside, the place felt foreign and cold.

She kept her coat on.

"Are you hungry?" her aunt asked, carefully removing her black veil and pulling off her gloves.

For a second, Eva felt like eating, but then she thought of her father starving to death in the lonely German countryside. Her appetite vanished.

"No," she responded.

"Tell me when you are."

"All right."

As Agnes disappeared into her room to take off that awful black dress, Eva trudged to her own quarters to do the same. When the girl finished, she peered into the empty hall. Then she pattered to her father's room and slipped inside.

It was stuffy in there, and dark. It smelled like an empty house.

Instantly, the child dashed across the room, tore the curtains apart, and flung open the window. A gust of warm air, salty and invigorating, surged in while the white autumn sun chased the shadows into the corners. Eva stared outside, watching the glittering puffs of foam leap up on the surface of the sea far off beyond the cliffs. Then she sank down onto her father's bed and curled her arms around one of its blue pillows.

The linen smelled like his cologne.

"Daddy," she groaned, feeling her throat constrict, "you can't imagine how much I miss you."

That night, as Eva lay in her father's bed with her face snuggled into that pillow, she tried once again to pretend that the last five days were all just a horrible dream.

❧

"Eva, get up."

Eva woke with a start and found her aunt standing over her. By the cloud-muffled morning sun leaking through the window, she saw that Agnes was already dressed.

"What is it?" Eva asked groggily.

"I'm off to the factory."

"So early?"

"Yes, I am Mr. Surrey's secretary full-time now. Don't you remember?" Agnes said, pulling the bedclothes off her niece. "You need to dress for school."

"Must I go today, Aunty?" the girl begged. "Yesterday was so horrid."

"Your grandmother didn't leave you the funds to go to a fine girls' school for nothing, Eva," Agnes said, handing her a robe. "I never had such an opportunity, but as long as I'm alive I shall make certain you go to that school every day its doors are open—whether you feel like it or not."

Eva knew arguing with her aunt was useless. After Agnes left

in from fixing the

for the factory, the girl grudgingly dressed, collected her things, and pedaled to the train station in the blustery October wind.

School that day was dreadful. Well-meaning teachers deluged her with their condolences throughout the day, and most of the other girls threw pity-filled glances in her direction every time she walked by. To another child this behavior might have been wonderfully encouraging, but at this stage of her sorrow, Eva wanted people to act as though nothing had happened.

Amanda Butterfield could not.

"Oh, it's just awful, Eva!" the short, flaxen-headed girl exploded when she saw Eva in the hall after their English period.

Eva winced as a knot of older girls turned to see what the noise was about.

"Mandy!" she hissed, glaring at her friend. "Don't shout!"

"Oh, I am sorry," Amanda said, her blue eyes watering. "It's just dreadful what's happened. I heard Mummy and Father talking about it last night when Father came in from fixing the sheep pins. Father said, 'Starbuck's gone, Maggie.' And Mummy said it was dreadful hard news. She'd heard it from Edna Quimpy at the hairdressers, but Carl Willis had told her—"

"Mandy, please," Eva interrupted. "I don't want to talk about it."

"Oh, dear, I'm sorry again," Mandy replied, puddling up afresh. "I just thought you would, because I know I would if it were my father who'd been killed so. I just couldn't keep it in, and that's a fact. I'd just die inside, I would, if I couldn't tell someone about how I felt."

"But I'm not you, Mandy," Eva said, trying with difficulty to be patient. "And thank you, but I just can't talk about it for a long time. Please, please don't say any more."

When the long day was over, Eva came back to a lonely house, tossed her bookbag inside the door, and sat on the front step, staring at the vacant cottage across the street.

"Hallo, Eva," someone said.

Wearily, Eva looked up. Harold York was standing beside her.

"Hallo, Harold," she returned, glancing up at him and wondering how someone only a couple years older than her could have grown so much taller in the past three years.

"It was a nice funeral," he said, plopping down beside her.

"Thanks."

"Nice as far as funerals go, I mean," he went on. "As far as anything else goes, I'd say it was rotten."

Eva smiled a little but said nothing. Several minutes passed while the children sat together on the step, staring at the empty house in front of them.

"Well," Eva said at length, "how is it?"

"How is what?"

"Having your father home," Eva replied.

"Oh. It's very nice."

"Harold," Eva said, turning to look at him, "you haven't told me a thing about your father all week. Is it really so nice?"

"Why, Eva, of course it is," Harold responded with surprise.

"Then tell me about it sometimes, please. I'm really very happy for you. If both our fathers had—oh, what I mean is, I'm not angry with you that your father came home and mine didn't," Eva said, struggling with the urge to cry. "Really, I'm not. I want to hear about how happy you and your parents are. It makes me happy, too. It reminds me that some stories do end well."

Harold said nothing for several moments.

"I'm sorry, Eva," he whispered. "I didn't realize."

"I didn't tell you," she said, rubbing her eyes.

"I'm sorry I can't think of anything helpful and nice to say," Harold sighed. "I tried a few things out on the way here, but they all sounded terribly stale. None of it was something I'd want someone else to say to me if I were you."

"That's all right," Eva returned, smiling for an instant.

"Well," Harold said, rising, "Dad and Mum and I are here when you happen to want us. Someone's home most all the time. If there's anything you ever need, you just tell us."

"Harold," Eva replied, "if I were me, that's exactly what I'd want someone to say."

The corner of Harold's mouth curled up into a bashful smile. Then he turned and started off down the street.

Chapter 4

"Six of them!" Mandy Butterfield cried, dancing through the carriage and dropping into an empty seat. "And one of them is the snowiest white you ever saw, Eva, with the shiniest black patches! Father says I may keep that one, as long as she does some herding when she's grown a bit."

"Well, congrats!" said Eva, sitting beside her friend on the homeward train and shoving her bookbag under the seat.

"You've got to come see all of Shelley's puppies, Eva. Do come today!" Mandy pressed as a few more girls from Southdale Girls' School clustered into the carriage.

"I can't today."

"Tomorrow, then!"

"Maybe the day after," Eva shook her head. "Tomorrow I'm going down to Cot's Pier with Harold. His father's buying a boat, you see."

"Cot's Pier?" said a high voice.

Eva and Mandy looked up to see a short, dainty girl of about fourteen standing in front of them. Twirling a dark, chocolatey brown lock of hair in one delicate hand, she stood looking down at them through her large hazel-tinted eyes with a countenance of polite hauteur. She was dressed in the same navy-blue uniform

31

the other girls wore, but somehow it was fancier on her. In fact, everything about her was uncommonly fancy and striking—and she seemed to know it.

"Oh," Eva mumbled. "Hallo, Priscilla."

"Hallo!" Mandy squeaked nervously.

"Going to Cot's Pier?" the other girl asked, taking the seat opposite them with the grace of a cultured woman and setting her expensive satchel and handbag beside her on the cushion.

The train hooted its horn twice to warn stragglers outside.

"Yes," replied Eva hesitantly. "Tomorrow."

"Why ever would you want to go down there?" Priscilla asked, her eyes widening with apparent concern.

"Why ever would I not?" Eva retorted as the engine lurched forward with one last toot of farewell.

"Well," Priscilla replied, lowering her voice and looking about. "It's such a common, ugly sort of place, Eva darling. Do you think your aunt would want you to go? Mother says she's rather a fine lady, so I'm sure she would want her niece to exhibit the same qualities."

Priscilla made these comments with such a compassionate tone that anyone who did not know her well would have interpreted her as the kindest, sweetest child on the face of the earth.

But Eva knew her well.

"My aunt, Priscilla," she said, her face burning, "doesn't care in the least that I go down to Cot's Pier tomorrow or any other day."

"Oh?" the other replied in her syrupy voice. "Well, that is nice."

"Priscilla, would you like to come see Shelley's babies tomorrow?" Mandy interrupted eagerly.

"Who is Shelley?" Priscilla asked.

"Our border collie," Mandy explained, beaming. "She had a litter of six just yesterday! And Father said I may keep the white one. You really must see her, Priscilla. Why, when she grows in all her fur, she's going to be even whiter than your collar!"

"Well, I'm afraid I don't much care for dogs," Priscilla returned, flashing another one of her captivating smiles, "or animals, really."

"I suppose," said Eva, turning from the window she had been staring through during the other girls' exchange. "I suppose you fine them much too common, eh?"

"Oh, certainly not!" gasped Priscilla, bringing her little white hand to her mouth.

"Or perhaps you find a girl who lives on a sheep farm rather mean company, then," Eva countered.

"Oh, Eva, don't!" Mandy exclaimed, her ever-ready supply of tears starting to leak out of her eyes. "How could you say that?"

"Because I know she's thinking it."

"Really, Eva darling!" Priscilla objected.

"Well, *I'm* not going to pretend," growled Eva, turning back to the window.

A moment of awkward silence followed before Mandy gathered courage to speak.

"Will you come, Priscilla?" she peeped.

"I'm afraid I can't. There is an important luncheon I must attend tomorrow with my parents."

"Well, I don't have any luncheons to attend," Eva declared. "I'll go and see Shelley's litter tomorrow, Mandy!"

Mandy's clouded face cleared at once, and her sunshiny expression resurfaced.

"Oh, lovely!" she cried. "But what about Harold?"

"Oh, I can see the boat another day," Eva said. "Cot's Pier will keep. Nothing much ever happens down there anyway."

❧

Harold York stood on the old Cot's Haven pier, with one hand wrapped about a post and the other shielding his dark eyes as he gazed across the water.

"Storm's coming," he announced. "Better hope Mr. Thurber comes with our boat soon."

"I'd rather he kept it 'til this blows over," his father said, eyeing the approaching tempest. "I haven't paid for it yet."

"Well," Harold reasoned, "he might have been here by now. It doesn't take that long from his dock. Looks like—say, Dad, there's a boat!"

"Certainly not ours," Mr. York snorted. "Where are your eyes, lad? Do you think your old dad would pay Thurber as much money as I'm about to for an old wooden wreck with an outboard engine?"

Mr. York motioned southeast to a little vessel jumping the choppy waves about a mile off.

"She's turning about like an undecided dog," Harold commented, looking more closely.

"No one's in her."

"How do you know?"

"If she's occupied, her pilot is drunk and lying in the hull, lad. We should see him if he were sitting up, and he certainly wouldn't be letting her have her head that way. The tiller must be unmanned."

The two watched in silence for a few minutes.

"Dad," Harold said eventually, "do you think the pilot is only drunk?"

"*If* there's a pilot," Mr. York corrected.

34

"If there is, then."

"I don't see anyone in her," he said at length, watching as the waves brought the craft closer to the pier. "Do you?"

"Not from here, no," Harold returned.

"Can't see past the gunwales. Of course, that doesn't mean someone is inside. I still say she's a derelict."

"What if she's not?"

"Then we're here," said his father simply, "and lucky for the pilot."

As the York men stared from the pier, the storm that had been brooding in the distance started to creep to the shore. The squall, it was clear, would outstrip the boat before the vessel reached the shore. Soon great rollers were rushing up behind the boat and curling about its sides.

Suddenly, less than half a mile away, one large wave struck the vessel from behind, tipping the stern into the air and exposing the interior of the boat.

"Dad!" Harold exclaimed, waving excitedly. "Look!"

For a long moment, time crawled. There was the stern held up by the wave. Then the boat was pointing straight into the air with its propeller spinning wildly atop it. Something dropped out. The next instant, the vessel slammed, keel-upward, into the water and was engulfed by the wave that struck it.

"Get a boat," Patrick York directed, tearing off his jacket, hat, and boots, "and meet me there."

Then Mr. York took a flying leap and dove off the pier. The boy stayed long enough to see his father pop out of the water and take off with a power stroke; then he dashed for the nearest dinghy, threw himself into it, yanked off her mooring line, and started the motor.

Despite the rough waters and his game leg, in just a few minutes Patrick York's excellent swimming abilities and powerful arms allowed him to reach the place where the boat had gone down. When Harold caught up with him a couple minutes later, he was diving in and out of the icy ocean around the vessel.

"Careful of the motor!" Harold yelled when his father surfaced again. "Did you find him?"

"Not yet!" Mr. York coughed, and disappeared.

Harold quickly scanned the waters around the boat, but he could see nothing. Soon his father's bedraggled head popped out alongside the boy's craft.

"Water's stirred up with so much sand and debris, I can't tell up from down," Mr. York spat.

Even so, he dove down three times more. Each time, he came up empty.

"What'll we do, Dad?" Harold asked as he helped his father into their boat.

By now it was raining buckets, and their craft was bounding up and down like a rocking horse ridden by a spirited toddler. Mr. York rubbed the water out of his eyes and glanced up at the sky.

"We'd better go back, lad," he said grimly. "Hand me the tiller."

The two men were silent on the way back to the dock. Even if they didn't have enough to occupy them with the storm and the rain, neither of them could think of anything to say. The man Harold had spotted in the overturning boat was gone; that was certain enough. There was nothing left to do but report what happened.

"Dad," Harold said when they had reached the pier and his father was tying down the line.

"Yes, lad?"

"Never mind," Harold replied, and he swallowed hard.

"You going to be all right?" his father asked, looking up from his work.

Harold bobbed his head firmly.

"Here, why don't you go and see if old Clint Fraser's boathouse is unlocked?" Mr. York suggested. "We can dry off and wait for the storm to blow over."

Harold agreed and started off down the pier. He had told his father he was going to be all right, and he was trying to convince himself of that. Determined not to do anything childish like start blubbing, he bit his lip and tried to look sturdy and confident. After all, men died every day. That was a fact of life. And if Harold York could not handle a fact of life, well then, for shame!

By the time he stepped off the pier, he had almost gotten a good handle on himself. Then he happened to glance down the beach at the waves thundering into the shore.

He lost himself completely.

"Oh, God! Dad! Someone help me!" he exploded, and he took off along the shore.

He didn't stop to see if his father had heard him. His eyes were glued to the place where he had seen something break out of an incoming wave.

"Help! Help!" he went on howling.

Soon he reached the spot and galloped into the water. He had not waded out more than a few yards before his leg bumped against an object. Swiftly, he seized it, tugged fervently, and found himself tumbling back into the surf.

"Someone help!" he shouted again, half-choking on a mouthful of ocean.

He got up and started to pull once more. Instantly his father was at his side, pulling too.

"Get him further up onto the beach!" Mr. York ordered.

"Further, further up! Away from the waves! Now, lay him down, lad!"

Harold dropped the arm he had been holding and looked down at the man they had dragged from the sea. His eyes still cloudy with water, the boy got only a vague impression of rags and red before his father was pushing the man onto his back and forcing water out of him.

"There's my handkerchief!" Mr. York barked, pausing an instant to fling his checkered kerchief at his son. "You get yours. Tie 'em together. Wrap it right there around his head. Hurry lad, he's bleeding hard."

His finger's trembling with adrenaline, Harold managed an awkward knot and clumsily tied the kerchiefs over the back of the man's head.

"Tighter, lad!" Mr. York ordered.

Harold made it tighter and then stood back out of his father's way. As thunder rumbled overhead, the boy looked anxiously up at the dark gray sky.

"Come on, come on," Mr. York growled, working the man's arms like a steam engine.

Little streams of water spurted intermittently from the man's mouth, but he never gave so much as a cough to show that he was alive.

"Come on, mate! Breathe! Try and breathe!" Harold's father panted earnestly.

Patrick York continued to work for sixty long seconds more, all the while pressing the man to not give up. Then at last he stopped and shook his head.

"What are you doing?" Harold gasped.

"It's no use," his father said, gently turning the man upon his back again. "Look at him. He's dead."

Harold gazed down at the man and felt his heart drop into

his boots. His father was right. The man's eyes were sunken into his ashen face, and every bone stuck out beneath his tattered clothing. His discolored hands and bare feet were missing several fingers and toes. That bruised, ocean-battered body looked like a castaway Harold had once seen depicted in a book.

The boy wondered if the man had been dead even before the boat overturned.

"Well," Mr. York said, rising to his feet.

Firming his chin, he heaved a sigh and stuck his hands into his pockets. Then, to his son's inestimable shock, Patrick York began to cry.

"Well," he said presently, clearing his throat and mastering himself again, "it's hard, that's for sure. I've seen too many men die in my life, son. After a while you stop getting hard to it and start getting soft again. Let's get him off the beach."

Bending down, he put an arm behind the dead man's head and under his shoulder.

"Now," he said, starting to raise him up, "on the count of three! One!"

Mr. York never got to three. Just as he was hoisting the body, the castaway unexpectedly lurched and let out a choking gurgle.

"My dear Lord!" Harold's father exclaimed. "The fellow's alive!"

As he spoke, the man burst into a fit of weak coughing intermingled with the most excruciating gasps. His eyelids rolled back halfway, and a shock of pale pink crept into his cheeks.

"It's all right, mate!" Mr. York cried, his face beaming. "Keep it up! Don't you stop it, now!"

"Shall I go get help?" Harold asked excitedly.

"What? Oh, yes, yes, and do it quickly, lad!" his father ordered, becoming serious again. "Run like the wind! He's not out of danger at all. Go!"

Harold turned and sprinted off for the village.

"We're getting help, mate," Mr. York said, carefully turning the man onto his side. "Just keep holding on."

The man rasped something in reply, but Mr. York could not make it out.

"What, now?" he said, bending down to his face. "Slowly now, mate."

Trembling, the man dug his hand into the shaley ground and whispered the one word that had struggled out of his salt-parched throat a moment before. Then his hand lost its grip and he slumped over in a faint.

Patrick York looked at him closely for a second.

"Oh, dear God," he breathed. "My God, help us."

Chapter 5

It was an eternal Thursday. Because her violin lessons were directly after school, Eva could not get home until past five in the afternoon. This happened every Thursday. It had happened this way for at least three years. Therefore, Eva was shocked by her aunt's reaction when she stepped through the front door at 5:15.

"Where in heaven's name have you been?" Agnes erupted, rushing into the hall.

"Why, music practice, Aunty," Eva exclaimed in surprise. "I always come home this late on Thursdays. You know that."

Her aunt threw up her hands and whirled round to walk away. Then she swiftly turned back and looked at Eva with the darting, fervent expression of a startled hen. It was then that Eva noticed her aunt's puffy nose and red eyes.

"Aunty," Eva said, setting her violin case and bookbag down, "what on earth is wrong?"

"Wrong?" Agnes piped.

"You've been crying, Aunty!"

"Nonsense! Now, keep your hat on! We're going out," Agnes ordered.

Agnes's hand was on the doorknob, and she was pulling it open.

Now Eva became truly scared. There stood her aunt, about to go out without hat or handbag, with her hair frazzled, her nose aglow, her lipstick faded. Never in Eva's life had she seen her aunt leave the house in such a state. Never. It was not just unheard of: it was incredible.

"Aunty," Eva said, her voice barely making it out of her mouth, "what is wrong?"

Agnes stopped and looked at Eva. She seemed on the verge of opening her mouth. Then she changed her mind, grabbed her coat out of the hall closet, snatched her handbag from the side table, and ushered her niece out the door.

Eva's aunt led her to their motorcar. That meant they were not going into Cot's Haven. The Starbucks never used the family car except to drive to another village or to the train station before a holiday. Feeling weak, Eva slid into the passenger seat next to her aunt. She wanted to ask again what was wrong, but now she was almost too scared to hear the answer.

They drove through Cot's Haven and passed the train station. Eva could not imagine where they were headed. Along the way, her aunt said nothing.

"Where are we going?" Eva asked after half an hour of complete silence.

"Eastbourne," her aunt replied tersely. "We're almost there."

"Aunty, I have a question."

"Not now, child," Agnes replied. However short she had been a moment ago, her voice now was strangely patient and almost tender.

Eva bit her lip and looked out the window. Soon they passed into the outskirts of Eastbourne and gradually maneuvered their way into the business section of the city. A couple blocks from St. Anne's Hospital, Agnes pulled into a carpark, paid the attendant, and drove their vehicle into the nearest space.

"Eva," she said, reaching forward and slowly turning off the ignition.

Eva looked at her. Her aunt was still staring straight ahead. Her lips were pursed. She was searching for words.

"Eva," Agnes said again, turning to face her niece, "I have something to tell you. Now, before I do it, you must promise me something. You've got to promise me you'll be as brave as you can. And if you can't be brave now, you must promise you'll keep trying to be until you are. All right?"

"I promise."

"Now, darling, remember how we couldn't find your father's— his body—in Germany?"

"Yes," Eva answered cautiously. Then an idea struck her: "Have they found him?"

Her aunt nodded her head hesitantly.

"Oh, Aunty, please!" Eva cried, panic assaulting her. "Please, Aunty, I can't see him! I can't! I couldn't bear it. *You've* got to identify him, Aunty. I couldn't!"

"Eva," Agnes said, her voice calm and persevering, "I didn't bring you here to look at a dead body. I wouldn't do such a thing to you."

"Then why are we here?" Eva asked, her chin still trembling.

"Darling, they didn't find your father's body in Germany," Agnes explained, "because he wasn't there."

"I don't understand."

"He didn't die in Germany as we were told, Eva. He didn't die anywhere."

Agnes took Eva's hand and squeezed it.

"Eva, your father isn't dead."

Eva felt like someone had just shoved her into a washing machine: everything started spinning. Then gradually, the world began to slow down again; and there was her aunt, sitting opposite her and still holding her hand.

"Daddy's alive?"

"Yes, child."

Eva sat in shocked silence, wavering between an explosion of joy and a bizarre feeling of numbness and unreality.

"Wait," she said at last, "if Daddy's alive, why did you make me promise to be brave?"

∽◌

Eva followed her aunt out of the lift onto the third floor of St. Anne's Hospital. How she was keeping her gelatinized legs from collapsing beneath her, she could not tell. She wanted to go somewhere and throw up.

"All right," Agnes said, halting before a door marked 318 and turning to her niece.

"Is he in there?" Eva asked, her stomach churning.

"He is," her aunt replied. "Now, remember what I told you."

"I'm scared," Eva hesitated. "I don't want to—I mean, I want—I don't know what I want."

"Eva," Agnes said, grasping the girl's shoulders and looking down at her tenderly, "it's all right. Whatever your father looks like now, he's still Ulysses Starbuck."

"Does he look anything like he did?" Eva questioned.

"Not much, no."

"I don't want to see him while he's awake, Aunty," Eva said. "Please, I don't. I'm afraid he'll see my face. I don't want to hurt him like that. I just can't."

"You don't have to. The nurse said he is asleep," Agnes said. "In fact, I haven't seen him awake yet."

Agnes opened the door and stepped inside. Eva lingered in the hall, trying to think of an excuse to delay this moment.

"Come along," her aunt said.

Her voice was patient but stern.

Eva dug her nails into her quaking palms and walked through the doorway.

There were two beds in the room. The cot nearest the door was empty. In the far wall of the room a large window allowed red streaks of fading autumn sunlight to pass through half-closed slats. This and a nearby lamp dimly illuminated a figure lying in the bed furthest from the door.

Eva stepped closer, her teeth sinking into her lip, her legs vibrating. In the bed lay a man more emaciated than the child had thought possible. His withered appearance was in peculiar contrast to his tall, broad frame. The back of his head was swathed in gauze, and his hollowed face was enveloped in an oxygen mask, through which the labored, uneven sounds of breathing could be heard.

Eva's gaze strayed from the man's head downward, absorbing the violence done to him in one sickened glance. Then she swiftly turned away.

"Aunty," she said through clenched teeth, "how could you think this is Daddy?"

"The doctors had several reasons," Agnes said, coming to the bed. "I just needed one."

Reaching over, she gently pushed a lock of brittle, white-tinged hair from the man's forehead. Underneath rested that same rose-colored angel mark Eva had kissed a thousand times over the years.

"Oh," Eva breathed.

Calmly, she brought a nearby chair to the side of the bed and sat down. She was silent for at least a minute, staring at the man in the bed. Somehow every scar or scrape, every tiny detail associated with pain on that figure, stood out with the deadliest clarity.

"What happened to his fingers?" the girl asked.

"Someone took them off, dear."

"The doctor?"

"No, Eva, someone else did," Agnes said hesitantly.

"Oh," Eva repeated in the same serene, collected tone she had been using. "Did they burn his arms, too?"

"Yes, Eva."

"That was very cruel of them, wasn't it?"

"Eva—"

"I'm fine," the child interrupted, standing up. "Really."

"Are you sure?" her aunt asked, looking askance at her.

"Positive," she replied. "Where is the powder room?"

"At the end of the hall and to the right," Agnes directed. "Do you want me to go with you?"

"No, I'll be right back," Eva said, heading for the door.

Eva inched down the hall, feeling as though she were treading through water. At length she reached the ladies' restroom. There was another woman there, a blonde, rosy-cheeked lady powdering her nose.

"Hallo," said Eva.

The lady smiled plastically at the girl before going back to her makeup.

Eva stood before the mirror, staring blankly at the pallid, freckled face and wide eyes that looked back at her from the other side. Eventually the blonde woman departed, leaving the girl alone with her reflection.

"Well," Eva told the girl in the mirror, "you're not very brave."

A few tears coursed down the other girl's face and dripped off her cheeks. Then all at once, the dam broke, and Eva sank down over the sink before her and wept.

No one in the hall heard the girl. Her cries were noiseless, the soundless sobs of a person aching so deeply that no word or cry is worthy enough to express it. At last, when no more tears would come, Eva wiped her eyes, pushed the hair out of her face, and left.

Sturdily, the girl walked back to Room 318. If she could not really be brave, she could at least pretend to be.

꘎

When Eva reached the room, she found her aunt at the door.

"There you are," Agnes said. "I was just off to look for you. The nurse was here a moment ago. She says I must go and sign some papers."

"Oh."

"Why don't you stay here until I come back?"

Eva would have preferred to go with her aunt, but she agreed anyway.

"Good girl," Agnes returned, giving Eva's shoulder a quick pat. "I will see you shortly."

Eva watched her aunt trot off down the hall. Then, taking a deep breath, she reluctantly went into Room 318.

The first thing she did was turn on another light and pull up the blinds to let in the last of the sun. The room was still too dim, but anything was better than the dark despair that hung about that place.

Hesitantly, timidly, the girl sat down beside her father. Then she reached out and took what was left of his hand and held it in hers.

It felt all wrong. It did not feel like her daddy's hand. It was cold, disfigured, smaller than she remembered. Eva squeezed that hand harder, fighting the impulse to drop it at once and dash out of the room.

Just then, Ulysses groaned and moved his head. Eva released her grasp, fearful that she had hurt him, and looked up at his face. Sluggishly, his eyes opened. They were still that beautiful green she had always remembered.

"Daddy?" Eva whispered, scooting herself closer to him.

He blinked and looked in her direction.

But he did not see her. He was looking past her. He might as well have been looking at the wall.

"Daddy, it's Eva," she said, touching his forehead with a trembling hand. "Say something to me."

His eyes focused on her face for just a moment. But there was no recognition and no emotion. There was nothing.

"Daddy, please," Eva pressed. "Please, it's Eva. Don't you remember me?"

Ulysses turned his head and stared vacantly out the window.

Immediately, Eva forgot all about pretending to be brave. The thought of her beloved father no longer recognizing her, his own daughter, was too much for her. Jumping to her feet, she rushed to the door and out into the hall, crying like a lost child.

"Blowed," Clint Fraser proclaimed, slamming down his mug to emphasize his point, "clean over, and no mistake. That's what I was, sirs. Saw the whole thing, I did—or most of it."

"So you've told us," grunted the barkeeper, swiping a towel across the splatter of beer that Fraser had sent shooting out of his drink. "And told us and told us."

"Not everyone's heard it, I'm sure, Barney," Fraser argued, jutting out his gray-stubbled chin and looking about the smoky interior of Mulchin's Pub. "Carter Tankard hasn't!"

Carter Tankard, a tall, wiry young man in his twenties, was seated at the bar a few stools away from the old sailor. Upon hearing his name, he turned politely to the man and adjusted his wire-rimmed spectacles.

"What haven't I heard?" he asked.

"My account on Ulysses Starbuck's insurrection," Fraser said.

"*Resurrection*," Barney corrected.

"Oh, yes, I heard it I'm sure," Carter bobbed his head. "You went down to your boathouse to see that the windows were shut, and Harold York came running past you. Is that it?"

"Yeah," Fraser acknowledged, a little crestfallen. "Who told you?"

"I read it in this morning's *Crier*," Carter revealed.

"Oh," said the other man. "Well, then."

"That's what happens when you tell the editor the whole tale, Clint," Barney interjected. "I understand Pat York was rather mum about the whole thing, so naturally they'd have to find a second-rate source."

"Mum he was!" Fraser readily asserted, having missed the barkeeper's insult. "Why, he knew all along that the man he'd pulled out o' the sea was Starbuck, but he didn't tell me a bit o' that, not even when I came and helped him take the chap to the boathouse to wait on the doc! I had to figure out the whole blasted thing later, I did. You'd think he didn't trust me!"

"My, but what a shock it's been," the bartender commented.

"Yes, and I hope a pleasant one," Tankard added.

"Pleasant?" Fraser restated. "Why wouldn't it be, eh? By heaven, man, to hear your loved one is alive and well again! How couldn't that be pleasant?"

"I heard he was in a dreadful state when they got him out," Tankard said after a thoughtful sip of beer. "Gone without air and all that, and other things. Well, what I mean is, sometimes there are much worse things than dying, mates. Or there are different ways to die and not really be dead. I'm sure each one of us who made it through the war knows what I mean. I just hope that it's a good thing, Starbuck coming alive again. I truly hope he wasn't better off really dead."

Chapter 6

"Next Friday," Agnes announced when Eva sat down for dinner.

"Next Friday?"

"Next Friday," her aunt continued, setting a dish of steaming shepherd's pie onto the table, "I'm going to Portsmouth Military Hospital."

"Oh," Eva returned.

"And I'm taking your father back home with me," Agnes concluded, eyeing her niece.

Eva looked up abruptly.

"That soon?" she exclaimed.

"It's been over a month," her aunt reminded her. "You've avoided your father long enough. I should have taken you to see him weeks ago, but I was too soft-hearted, knowing how you felt. Now he will be here in less than ten days, and you aren't at all prepared."

"Aunty, you don't understand! He doesn't remember me!"

"How do you know? You haven't seen him in weeks."

"Well, does he remember you?"

"No," Agnes admitted, taking her seat. "But he wasn't calling my name when Patrick York dragged him out of the Atlantic."

Eva looked down at her lap and furrowed her auburn brows.

"I know this is difficult for you, Eva," Agnes said. "Don't think it is easy for me. Ulysses is my brother just as much as he is your father. Every time I visit Portsmouth, I tell myself I can't go back, that I can't stand seeing him that way again. But I know that I must. We will not put him in a nursing home, Eva. I refuse to."

"Oh, never!" the girl affirmed, her head jerking up again. "I would never want that!"

"I know. But don't you see that if we won't send him there, we must take him with us?"

"I want him with us!" Eva answered. "I want to see him again. I haven't stayed away from the hospital all this time because I don't want to. I really do want him, Aunty. I just want *him*. I don't care what he looks like on the outside, as long as he's inside.

"But he's not there anymore. It's like he's away. His body's there, but Daddy isn't. I can't stand it. It's terrible to see him like that."

"Eva," her aunt replied, that kind note emerging from her voice again, "I know you don't like this. I don't either. You know Dr. Neilson explained that Ulysses may always be like that, after what happened in the Nazi camp, the boat striking his head when it overturned, and all the time he went without air before he was pulled out of the water. It's all very bad. We're lucky he's alive at all.

"But the doctor also said there is a chance of him recovering some part of himself. And the only way Dr. Neilson believes this can happen is if we bring Ulysses home. We can't expect him to get any better in the hospital or a nursing home or—or other places. Here, with people whom he knew and loved about him continually, there is a chance. It's just a little one, mind, but it's a chance I believe we should give him. Don't you?"

"Of course, Aunty."

"Friday next, then," Agnes said, dipping a spoon into the pie.

"Yes," Eva said, firming her chin, "Friday next."

The unexpected reappearance of Ulysses Starbuck was the talk of Cot's Haven for at least two weeks after the day Harold York stampeded into Mulchin's Pub looking for the local physician. Even so, by the third week the topic had fallen out of casual pub conversation. When a month had passed, not even Clint Fraser and the rest of the village idlers thought of discussing it. There were other matters of more contemporary interest to be debated, such as the Soviet Union and the unforeseen marriage of the Vicar Farrier's daughter to the undertaker.

Despite Cot's Haven's fading attention to the matter, it was still a pressing case for Major Arnold, a man who took his job very seriously. Although he was disturbed that he had been a part of erroneously announcing a man's death, there were other things about the case that were more troubling to him.

Soon Arnold found Marvin Short and called him to his office to explain himself. Short maintained that Starbuck's return was as much a shock to him as to everyone else and was adamant that he had thought the sergeant dead before he left him.

"I tell you, he was my best mate!" he swore again. "I'd never have walked off if I wasn't sure he was gone. I can't tell you how it tears me up to think I went and left him there alive. It was a horrible mistake, it was, but that's *all* it was."

Eventually, pressured by a lack of evidence, the major accepted the young man's explanation. As dissatisfied as he was with the case, there was nothing else to do. The only other person who was present when Short abandoned his sergeant was Starbuck himself, and he was in no condition to shed light on the matter. There were no grounds to warrant further investigation.

"Well," he told himself as he set Starbuck's case file aside and moved on to other matters. "All a man can do now is keep his eyes open."

And luckily, he did.

∽⌀∾

Sometimes it is much easier to be brave about something when it is in the future where one can forget about it. All through the mid-November week that lay between one Friday and the next, Eva managed to convince herself that her father's return was nothing to be frightened of. She prayed about it a little and felt better—not so much because she had prayed but because Friday was off in the distance and easy to ignore.

Then came Friday. It was a dreadful day from the start. The rain soaked Eva's clothes and hair before she could reach the train station. She found she had forgot a textbook and then discovered Mandy Butterfield was ill and not there to share hers. Before the morning was through, she received an abominable mark on an English exam. Later, when the rain cleared, the teachers decided there really was no reason to cancel the photographer's appointment to take a picture of all the girls in front of the school. Eva did not want to imagine what future generations at Southdale Girls' School would say about her stringy hair and frazzled face. Finally, as if to crown the sorry day, just before Eva's beloved music period, the headmaster released all the girls an hour early to combat the stomach illness that was spreading through the school.

By the time the 2:47 train chugged up to the platform near Cot's Haven, it had begun to rain again. Eva cycled home in soaked stockings, drooping hat, and dripping hair, grateful that Harold was not there to tactlessly laugh at her revolting appearance and call her a water rat. When she reached the front door, saturated enough to have taken a bath in all her clothes, she was past caring about her condition.

After shoving the door open, Eva stepped into the hall and peeled off her coat, hat, and rubbers.

"Aunty!" she called, shaking her coat off at the mat. "The headmaster let us leave early! I'm soaked through."

Eva turned to hang up her coat—and shrieked.

There was nothing to scream over. Eva saw that as soon as the cry left her lips. But since a moment ago she had been alone in the hall, she really didn't expect to turn and find her father standing next to her.

"Eva, what's wrong?" her aunt questioned, appearing in the sitting room doorway.

"I—um—" Eva stuttered, looking up at her father.

Again, he was not looking at her. Instead, he was staring vacuously down at the sodden coat she held in her hands. But he was standing, and his face was not nearly so pale, and he must have gained at least fifteen pounds since she had last seen him.

"Daddy?" she said.

Ulysses turned and shuffled past Agnes into the sitting room.

"What happened, Eva?" her aunt asked.

"He startled me. I didn't know he was there. Did the hospital bring him here early?"

"Yes, a few hours early," her aunt informed her. "Thankfully, Mr. Surrey gave me the whole day off. You're soaked through, Eva."

Eva looked down at herself.

"I am."

"You'd better take a hot bath and get something warm on," Agnes directed.

"He didn't remember me," Eva said.

"Eva, he only just arrived. He doesn't remember hardly

anything. He hasn't said a word. He's very detached from his surroundings. We can't expect too much out of him, especially on his first day home in six years. Now run along," she added. "You need a bath."

Before the day was over, a nurse named Grace Watkins came to the Starbuck cottage to take a position helping Eva's father. At first, when her aunt told her about the arrival of this new addition to their home, Eva offered nothing but protest.

"We don't need any nurse!" she contended. "We can take care of Daddy ourselves! You said he can eat and dress himself and do most everything on his own. Why do we need her?"

"Eva," Agnes answered with a dangerous edge in her voice, "I will be gone most of every weekday at the factory. You will be away at school until at least four. That leaves your father home alone for eight hours. I refuse to leave a confused relative by himself for that long."

"Aunty!"

"Enough," Agnes barked. "Miss Watkins has gone to a great deal of trouble to come live in Cot's Haven and look after your father. I watched her care for him while he was at St. Anne's, and I am entirely confident in her abilities."

Although initially Eva still held strong reservations, her dislike dissipated soon after she met Miss Watkins.

Never had she seen such a sweet smile on anyone's face. Grace was a short, slightly plump, apple-cheeked young woman in her mid-twenties, with wavy brown hair and bright, kind green eyes nearly the same color as Ulysses'. Her voice was high and still rather girlish; yet she seemed to possess an emotional maturity and personal charm that allowed her the unique ability to be friends with someone of any age.

In the weeks to come, Eva and her aunt would develop an

even higher opinion of the young nurse. But Eva would eventually discover that not all nurses were quite so trustworthy.

Eva was right that her father could do almost anything on his own. Despite his emotional and mental departure from reality, he maintained a fragmented awareness of certain things around him. For instance, the sound of a voice seemed lost upon him, but a touch on the shoulder would elicit a sudden jerk. While he never appeared to see people, the placement of a shirt upon his bed could motivate him to dress himself. He knew where the sofa was to sit on, but he didn't know that Grace sat on it with him.

Most of Ulysses' existence was painfully passive: move only if moved. Individuals were forces pushing him toward certain actions, and he obeyed with no more thought than a tree responding to the draw of the sun or the push of the wind. He never spoke; he never smiled; his eyes were never in focus. Ulysses Starbuck was not at home, and it was no good leaving a message.

"Tomorrow is Sunday," Eva said one evening as she and her aunt were relaxing by the sitting room fireplace.

"So it is," Agnes replied without looking up from her book.

"Daddy and I always went to church on Sundays," Eva said.

Agnes's eyes drifted upward and peered at her niece over the black rims of her reading glasses. The flames from the hearth flickered at Eva from the lenses.

"What of it?" Agnes asked.

Eva glanced over at the sofa on the other side of the room, where her father sat with his head leaned back on the cushion, staring up at the ceiling plaster.

"Well," Eva returned, dragging out the word, "I think Daddy would want to keep attending."

"Are you suggesting," Agnes questioned, lowering her book and taking off her spectacles, "that we take your father to church in the morning?"

"Well, yes."

"And naturally I am included in *we*."

"If you don't mind," Eva replied, nervously noting the muscles tensing around her aunt's thin lips. "I don't think I could handle him myself."

"You do realize that I haven't gone to any church since you were born," Agnes said, her voice hardening.

"But for Daddy, you might go."

Agnes closed her book with a bang that made Eva jump in her seat.

"No," she said icily. "I never approved of your father's ideas, and I will not start approving of them even now."

"But," Eva pleaded, "he did so love going!"

"Exactly," Agnes shot back, her volume rising. "And what good has that done him? This religion of your father's didn't profit him a single thing, did it? There he sits—"

Abruptly, Agnes stopped herself.

"Never mind," she concluded, flipping her book open again. "I won't go and he won't, so that's settled."

For a few seconds, Eva sat in stunned silence.

"I want to go," she murmured after swallowing the lump that had formed in her throat.

"Go on then," Agnes replied. "The Yorks will be here to take you in the morning anyway."

"I want Daddy to go with us sometime."

"The Yorks have better things to worry about," Agnes

objected. "They've done enough for us; I won't ask them to look after your father."

"Sometime, Aunty," Eva pushed, gazing at her imploringly. "Please."

Agnes glanced up at her and turned a page in her book. The conversation was over.

"Eva," Agnes said a few minutes later.

"Yes?"

"Go to bed."

Eva stood and left the sitting room. When she returned, she was in her nightgown.

"Good night, Aunty," she said.

"Mm-hm," Agnes muttered, turning another page.

Eva walked to the sofa and touched her father's arm. Ulysses gave a start and pulled away.

"Good night, Daddy," the girl whispered.

Then she went to bed. She had wanted to kiss him good night as she used to, but she was too afraid. She felt she could not bear it if he pulled away from that.

The next day, Eva could see that her aunt was still miffed about their conversation from the previous night. Before Eva left with the Yorks, Agnes was short (or shorter than usual) with her words and frosty in her tone. When the girl returned, the lady was hardly more pleasant.

"Jolly time, I suppose?" were her first words when Eva walked into the kitchen.

"It was nice," Eva replied. "Did you have a nice morning?"

"Certainly," Agnes said dryly, punching down a bowl-full of dough.

"All right. What's that you're making?"

"Dinner rolls," Agnes grunted, slapping the dough onto the table and working it with her long, slender fingers.

"When shall we have them?"

"At dinner," Agnes said. "It's a nice time for dinner rolls, you know."

"Oh. When are we eating lunch?"

"Whenever you like," her aunt informed her, "since you will be preparing it."

Eva paused to ponder her aunt's words.

"Aunty," she said at length, "was it such a bad day?"

"What makes you think it was?" Agnes asked, wadding up the dough and dropping in back into the bowl with a thud.

"You always have lunch ready by now," Eva explained. "Oh, I don't mind if it's not, you understand, but the fact is you always do. And the last time you asked me to prepare a meal was when you had pneumonia two years ago."

"Well," Agnes said, "you're right. It was a rotten day."

"Daddy?"

"Yes."

"How so?"

"Never mind," Agnes replied. "Suffice it to say he doesn't want a shave and will be growing a beard."

"Well, that's fine. I think he'll look nice with a beard, don't you?"

Her aunt snorted.

"Where is he?" Eva asked.

"Still in bed, I suppose. I'm sure he's exhausted after the battle we fought this morning. Hasn't eaten or drunk a thing, too. Come to think of it, neither have I!"

"I'm sorry, Aunty."

"No more than I," grumbled Agnes.

After putting some sandwiches together, Eva went to her father's room to wake him for lunch. As she stole into the room, she noticed the place was still darkened by the window's heavy navy-blue curtains. Ulysses, stretched out amidst a mess of sheets and pillows, lay insensible to the world.

Eva gave a determined sigh and gently shook her father's shoulder.

"Daddy, wake up."

He must have been remarkably exhausted, for it took several hearty shakes and a shout to wake him. When aroused, he groaned in protest and pulled a pillow over his head like a child avoiding a school day.

"Daddy, you need to eat," Eva said, tugging on his arm.

After a little more persuasion, Ulysses pushed himself into a slumped sitting position and shivered. He was nearly as disheveled as his bed: dark circles sagged under his eyes, his wrinkled shirt was buttoned all wrong, and his hair stood up in several places.

Since the fire Agnes had built a few hours before was now dead, Eva grabbed her father's robe from a bedpost and draped it over his shoulders.

"All right, come along," said the girl, taking Ulysses by the hand.

All Eva did was grasp his hand. It was a gentle action, not a sudden seizure or blow. Eva certainly was not expecting her father to be unsettled by the gesture. But instantly, Ulysses twisted his hand out of hers and shoved Eva away with his other arm.

Eva was too stunned to cry out. She had the sensation of falling backward and then felt a sharp pang as her head struck something behind her. The next moment, she blacked out.

Chapter 7

Eva could not have been unconscious more than a minute, for when she awoke on the floor, her father was in the same position in which she last remembered him. There was a beastly pounding in her ears, and white sparks dotted her vision. Shakily, she reached her hand up and felt the back of her head. It was warm and wet.

Oh no, she thought. *I'm bleeding!*

Stunned, she gripped the arm of the chair behind her with one hand and gradually sat up. With an effort, she got to her feet and stood a dizzy moment holding on to the chair.

"Aunty," she said weakly.

Realizing her aunt could not hear her from the kitchen, Eva staggered out of the room into the hall.

"Aunty!" she called more loudly.

"What is it, Eva?" Agnes yelled. "I'm busy!"

"Aunty," Eva said, leaning against the wall, "I'm bleeding!"

In three seconds, Agnes was there.

"Eva!" she gasped. "What happened? Don't move! Hold on while I get a towel."

Agnes returned speedily and guided Eva into the sitting

room. After leading her to the sofa, Agnes pulled the girl's hand away and pressed the towel down onto her head.

"How do you feel?" she asked anxiously.

"A little dizzy. My head hurts," Eva mumbled, looking down at her hand. "I'm bleeding."

"Shush," Agnes ordered. "I'm going to call Dr. McCabe."

"Oh, I'll be all right."

"After he examines you, you will," Agnes answered. "Now put both of your hands on this towel. There. Press as hard as you can, and don't move."

With that, Agnes hurried to the telephone in the kitchen.

While Eva was pushing down on her head, the initial shock began to wear off. Until this moment, she had not considered how she had struck her head; she had been far too busy trying to grasp that she *had* hit it. Now the events leading to her fall started pouring into her thoughts.

"Aunty!" she cried.

"I'm coming!"

"Please hurry!"

Agnes rushed into the room.

"Dr. McCabe is coming," she said. "He says you're to sit still."

"Aunty," Eva repeated, looking wild-eyed up at her.

"What is it, dear?"

"Daddy did it!"

"He what?"

"He shoved me back," she explained through sudden tears, "and I fell and hit my head on the chair."

"Eva darling, do you know what you're saying?" Agnes questioned.

"Yes!"

"Why did he push you?"

"I don't know! It happened so fast! Daddy did it, Aunty! My daddy did it!"

When Dr. McCabe arrived several minutes later, Agnes took the opportunity to go to Ulysses' room. She found him sitting where Eva had left him. He did not appear angry or afraid. On the contrary, he was almost asleep.

"Ulysses!" Agnes hissed, grasping his arm. "How could you?"

Her brother shivered and let out a coughed.

Without a word, Agnes whisked off Ulysses' robe and gently pushed him back into the bed. Then she put a couple blankets over him, built up the fire, and left the room.

"No school for the rest of the week," Dr. McCabe was saying when Agnes returned. "Once I finish with this bandage, you're to spend the next seven days resting quietly like a good girl. Don't upset yourself and don't be running about."

"Yes, sir," Eva wincing as the doctor pulled the bandage tight.

"Now, how did this happen?" he asked.

"She tripped and hit her head on a chair," Agnes said. "Right, Eva?"

Eva glanced at her aunt.

"Right," she agreed.

Dr. McCabe, a short, thin man with white hair the thickness of a newborn's, shifted his glasses further up his nose and frowned.

"Well!" he said after a pause. "Most unfortunate."

"How is she, doctor?" Agnes asked.

"She's got a nasty cut and a mild concussion," McCabe said, wiping his hands on a cloth. "However, her skull is made of sterner stuff. She should be in mint condition again in a couple weeks, if she keeps quiet as I told her and, of course, avoids troublesome chairs."

"I'm sure she will."

"Do call me if anything should change," the doctor directed. "Now, if you'll allow me to use your tap, I'll be on my way."

∽◌

Grace Watkins arrived, whistling, at exactly seven the next morning. Faced with the early hour and the events that had taken place the previous day, Agnes found the nurse nauseatingly punctual and cheerful. After giving her a brief report on Eva's condition (minus the cause) and stating that she intended to pay the girl extra for looking after Eva, Agnes mounted her cycle and pedaled off rather earlier than needed.

Eva awoke to the tune of "Greensleeves" being whistled nearby. Groggily, she rolled out of bed, threw on her robe and bedroom slippers, and stumbled out of her room.

"Why, hallo Eva!" Grace piped from Ulysses' doorway across the hall.

"What time is it?" Eva asked, rubbing her eyes.

"Half past eight at least," Grace informed her.

"That early?" Eva groaned.

"I thought you got up at half past seven during the week," Grace said with a smile.

"As far as I'm concerned, it's Saturday," Eva grumbled.

"Well, I'm sorry to rouse you. And I'm sorry about your accident. How are you feeling?"

"I've got a beastly headache, but I'm all right. Are you waking my father up?"

"Why, yes," Grace replied. "Breakfast in twenty minutes. Are you hungry?"

"Um," Eva said, feeling her stomach growl its assent, "no, not now. A little later."

"Say, after your father eats?" Grace asked with a meaningful glance.

"Sure, maybe," Eva said, turning and making a hasty exit back into her room.

She had not lain in bed long, in sheer torture from the smell of ham, before Grace knocked on the door and poked her head in.

"Has he finished already?" Eva asked hopefully.

"No, he's a little slow in rising this morning. You have a visitor."

"What? Who?"

"A tall, handsome young fellow," said Grace with a wink.

"I don't know any tall, handsome young fellows."

"Well, this one has brown hair and eyes and says his name is—"

"You're not talking about Harold, are you?" Eva interrupted.

"Yes, that's the name. Don't you think he's a sweet one?"

"But Harold!"

Grace laughed.

"Well, he's in the sitting room," she said. "Don't keep him waiting."

Eva wriggled into her robe again and marched out into the hall. When she reached the sitting room, Harold jumped up from the sofa, his hands behind his back.

"Hallo, Eva!" he greeted. "My, you look awful this morning!"

"I do my best," Eva grunted. "Did you risk missing school to tell me that?"

"No, not exactly," Harold replied. "This won't take but a minute."

"What won't?"

"What I've come for, of course."

"Well, what is it, then?"

Coloring like a beet, Harold brought something out from behind his back.

"Oh, carnations!" Eva exclaimed.

"Yes," Harold said, handing the flowers over as swiftly as if they were aflame.

"Yellow's my favorite color," Eva revealed after breathing deeply. "Thank you, Harold! You shouldn't have."

"Oh, they're from all of us," Harold replied, turning red again. "From Mum and Dad and me. We hope you feel better soon."

"Do tell your parents thank you for me."

"Of course," Harold said, snatching his cap from the arm of the sofa. "Well, I'm off."

"Drop by soon, Harold. This week I'll be bored enough to talk even to you."

Harold snickered and put on his cap.

"Say, what did you trip over to knock your head that way?" he asked.

Eva's face clouded.

"I don't know," she said.

"Tripped over that myself," the boy smirked.

"Get out," Eva returned with a grin.

When Harold had gone, Eva's smile evaporated, and she dropped onto the sofa. Soon Grace came back to the room.

"Feeling all right?" she asked.

"A bit dizzy."

"Still hungry?"

"Ravenously!" Eva chirped before she could remember she was not supposed to be. "I mean, I am now."

"Ah, I see."

"Grace," Eva said, "can I tell you something?"

"Certainly."

"Oh, well, not now," Eva stammered. "I've forgotten."

"Well, if you want to tell me, I'll be around," said the nurse. "In the meantime, how would you like your breakfast in bed this morning?"

"Very much. Thanks."

❧

For the next three days, Eva avoided her father. She could hardly bear to be in the same room with him for long, let alone to tell him good night. Aside from a new stubborn but silent resistance which Grace patiently struggled to overcome, Ulysses showed no signs of aggression or change in behavior. Still, Eva stayed away from him, and this behavior worried her aunt.

Agnes tried to reason with Eva, reminding the girl of her father's condition and insisting that Ulysses couldn't have known what he was doing when he pushed her.

"Eva," Agnes insisted, "if your father had any inkling of what he did to you, I can't imagine the grief it would cause him. He loved you so very much."

"But he doesn't love me now," Eva replied.

"Eva! How can you say that?"

"He doesn't, Aunty. He doesn't love *anyone* anymore. He couldn't. How can you love someone you don't remember?"

Agnes did not respond. How could she? After all, she had never forgotten anyone she loved.

Chapter 8

"Surprise!" Mandy Butterfield cried, popping her head over the garden wall.

Eva, who had been lazily soaking in the afternoon sun, nearly choked on her tea.

"Mandy!" she coughed.

"Yes!" the other girl giggled, dashing round the wall and entering through the garden gate.

In her arms she carried a bundle of white and black fur.

"You didn't bring Daisy!" Eva exclaimed, setting down her tea and eagerly taking the little border collie pup from her friend.

"I did indeed," said Mandy. "Carried her in my bicycle basket the whole way! Oh, all during the week I wanted to come see you, but Mummy said you were resting, and I oughtn't to bother you."

"Oh, I wasn't that ill," Eva said, stroking the puppy's black ears.

"We didn't know," Mandy explained, settling upon the stone bench beside her friend. "Are you better now?"

"Much. I can go back to Southdale on Monday."

"Oh, keen!" Mandy beamed. "Things are dreadful without you. But Eva, it's so cold out here! How do you stand it?"

"I suppose we should go in," Eva muttered reluctantly. "But let's go to my room. It's more comfortable in there."

"That's perfect!" said Mandy, skipping ahead to the kitchen door. "You can see the house across the street from there."

"What does that matter?" Eva asked, following the other girl inside.

"Eva, don't you know?" Mandy answered, waving her arms. "You are the luckiest girl in the whole village!"

"Me?"

"Yes! Here, let's look through the window seat in your sitting room," Mandy suggested. "The view is much better from there."

"Um, Mandy!" Eva started, but it was too late: her bubbly companion was already bouncing down the hall.

Hoisting the dog further up in her arms, Eva trailed after her friend.

"It's a fantastic spot," Mandy was saying as she stepped into the sitting room. "We can both get—oh!"

The girl halted abruptly.

"Hallo, Mr. Starbuck," she said, at once becoming shy.

Eva's father, in his usual place on the sofa, did not acknowledge the greeting.

"He can't hear you," Eva said.

"Oh, dear, I didn't know," Mandy replied, her ears reddening. "Are you sure?"

"Quite," Eva returned dryly. "Or he doesn't usually."

"I'm sorry," Mandy said, wringing her hands in front of her. "I don't know much about all this."

"Well, I didn't tell you anything," Eva said. "Let's go to my room."

"I *am* sorry," Mandy said as the girls stepped into Eva's bedroom. "When I heard your father was alive, I thought it was like it was my father. There was a little time in hospital, but when

70

he came home, everything went back to normal. Father is still rather cross over losing part of his arm, it being so inconvenient and all. But he's still himself."

"I thought it would be that way, too," Eva sighed, sitting down on her bed, "a long time ago. I thought we'd get him back and everything would just be the way it was. But it didn't turn out that way. We didn't get him back."

"What do you mean?"

"I mean he's not here," Eva said, blinking away a tear. "I can tell every time I look at him. He's all dark inside now, and the sun won't come there. And I just can't stand it, Mandy. All the good parts of him are gone, like a box of chocolates that's empty. And all we've got left is that dark box! Oh, I'm not making any sense!"

Mandy sat beside her friend and passed her a pink kerchief. Then, without warning, she let out a sob and started to cry even harder than Eva.

"What's wrong?" Eva sniffed.

"I don't know!" Mandy moaned. "It's just awful! If I were you, I'd be the most unhappiest girl in the village!"

"I thought you said I was the luckiest one," Eva reminded her.

"Oh, I did."

Eva smiled and handed the girl back her kerchief.

"I can't talk about this anymore," she said. "Why don't you show me why I'm so lucky, eh?"

"Yes!" Mandy exclaimed, breaking into a radiant grin. "Come to the window!"

Eva set Daisy down on her bed and hurried to the window with her friend.

"There!" Mandy said, pointing triumphantly across the street.

"All I see is the empty house," Eva replied, straining her eyes.

"You silly thing, it's not empty anymore! Didn't you know a family took it a week ago?"

"I didn't. But why does this make me so fortunate?"

"Because it's occupied by the dreamiest fellow you'll ever see!" Mandy revealed, clutching her hands together and rolling her eyes heavenward. "Their name's Wyatt, and their son is called Roger—doesn't that sound manly?—and he's the talk of Southdale, Eva!"

"Oh, pooh!" Eva laughed. "So was your brother Ira after he saved Chelsey Court from that speeding lorry a couple years ago. No one says a thing about him now."

"But Roger's different, Eva. He's delicious!"

Eva was just about to reply when the front door of the other house opened.

"It's him!" Mandy squeaked, pressing her nose to the glass.

Eva had planned on a rebuttal against her friend's elevated opinion of the new boy, but when she actually saw Roger Wyatt, the words vanished from her brain.

"Ooooh," she breathed, leaning forward.

"Look at that hair, that jaw, those eyes!" panted Mandy.

"It's so blonde," Eva said.

"It's so firm!"

"They're so big!"

"I'm going to die!" Mandy concluded.

"Oh, but he must be too old," Eva mentioned, watching the boy wheel a bicycle to the curb. "He's much too tall."

"Only sixteen," Mandy said.

"Only? Do you realize how old that is, Mandy? We're only twelve!"

"Almost thirteen," Mandy corrected. "Father was twenty-three when he married Mummy, and she was only nineteen."

"Yes, but she was nineteen, not twelve," Eva argued.

"I don't care," Mandy returned. "He's such a dish!"

As she spoke, the boy looked up and saw the girls peering

at him from the window. Smiling to show a beautiful row of snow-white teeth, he waved at them, hopped onto his cycle, and sped away.

"He waved at us!" Mandy all but screamed, clapping her hands together.

Eva said nothing as her friend danced about the room, but inside she was wondering if Mandy might not be right. Just then, she really did feel like the luckiest girl in the village.

Eva was in a deep sleep, dreaming blissfully of cycling through Cot's Haven with Harold before the war. The house was still. Outside the only noises were the muffled boom of the waves on the beach, the dry rustling of dead leaves still clinging to their branches, and the occasional call of a night bird. Everything was peaceful.

Thunk!

Eva turned over and mumbled to herself.

Thunk!

Abruptly, the girl awoke and sat up in bed.

Thunk, thump.

The noise was not very loud, but it was certainly coming from within the house. Noiselessly, Eva hopped out of bed, tiptoed to her door, and stuck her head out into the hall.

Thump, thunk, went the sound.

It was coming from her father's bedroom.

Forgetting her slippers, the girl crept with frigid feet down the hall and eased her father's door open. The room was dim, but a spray of moonlight peeped in through the window. Ulysses' bed was empty.

Thunk.

Eva's flesh was crawling. Turning, she darted down the hall and slipped into her aunt's room.

"Aunty!" she hissed into the darkness.

"Mmm," came the reply.

"Aunty, wake up!"

"Mmm, what is it? Eva?"

"Yes!"

The bed creaked.

"Eva, what are you doing up at this hour?"

"I think there's something wrong with Daddy."

"What do you mean?"

"I don't know. He's not in his bed, and I keep hearing—"

Thunk!

"Where is that coming from?" Agnes questioned, throwing off her coverlet.

"Daddy's room."

Agnes stumbled to her feet and grabbed the poker from the hearth.

"Stay here," she instructed.

"Yes, Aunty," Eva breathed. "But please be careful!"

"Shh!" Agnes said with a warning finger on her mouth.

Eva's aunt sneaked out of the room and into the hall. As she reached Ulysses' door and peered in, the dull thumping noise was joined by a scraping sound. Gripping the poker firmly in her hands, Agnes stepped into the room.

Ulysses' bed was still unoccupied.

Thump!

Agnes's heart leapt into her mouth, but she managed to take a couple more steps, her head whisking around in search of the noise's source. In the stillness that followed the thump, the sound of heavy breathing could be heard. It was coming from Ulysses' closet.

Agnes inched up to the closed door.

Thunk! came the noise from behind it.

"Who's in there?" Agnes called. "Ulysses?"

There was no response but the rustle and bump.

"Who's there?" the lady repeated, raising her voice. "Well then, you asked for it!"

Swiftly, Agnes fumbled for the light switch on the wall and turned the knob, illuminating her brother's room. Then she seized the brass handle and shoved against the closet door. But the door only opened a crack; she felt resistance from the other side.

"Come out!" she ordered, her voice unnaturally high.

In reply, a hand shot out from within, clutched the edge of the door in a claw-like grip, and started to pull the door back.

Agnes raised the poker high and prepared to strike. Even as she did, the door swung inward, and her brother tumbled out.

"Oh, my heavens!" Agnes gasped, throwing the weapon aside and bending down. "Ulysses!"

Her brother was trembling all over. His brow was beaded in sweat; his eyes darted wildly back and forth. Fearful that something or someone had frightened Ulysses this badly, Agnes snatched the poker again, lunged forward, and pulled the string to the closet light.

The room was a wreck. Strewn with clothing and debris, the floor was blocked by the entire contents of the closet's small chest of drawers, including the drawers themselves. On the rack overhead, several clothes hangers were still swinging back and forth, thumping against the wall behind them. One of the panels at the back of the closet was half-pried loose.

But there was no one and nothing else inside.

"Aunty?" piped a shaky voice from the hall.

"It's all right," Agnes said, once again tossing the poker away.

Eva sprinted into the room.

"What's happened?" the girl cried. "What's wrong with Daddy?"

Ulysses was still panting on the floor, but he was not shaking so violently.

"I don't know," Agnes shook her head, grasping her brother's hand and patting his shoulder.

"He looks awful. Should we call the doctor?"

"No!" Agnes snapped. "There is no reason to. You see he is already calming down. I'll just wedge the closet door open and help him back to bed."

"But why was he so frightened?"

"I don't know! Now go to bed, Eva!"

Unwillingly, Eva left her aunt and went back to her room.

"It's all right, brother," Agnes assured him when the girl had gone. "You're going to be fine. Don't worry. I won't let the doctor come. We both know what he would do. And I'm never going to let that happen to you."

⌒⌒

Agnes was awakened by someone tapping on her shoulder. "Miss Starbuck?"

"What?" Agnes cried, sitting up in her chair.

"You're in your brother's room," Grace said, bending over her. "Miss Starbuck, what happened here last night?"

"How did you get in here?" Agnes returned angrily. "Where's my brother?"

"He's over there in his bed," Grace said. "I rang the bell, but when no one came to the door, I let myself in with the key you gave me. That's when I found Mr. Starbuck."

"Where?"

"He was lying on the sitting room rug. He was clearly

exhausted, so I took him to bed," Grace continued. "Miss Starbuck, what happened?"

"Nothing," Agnes lied.

Then she changed her mind.

"I mean, I don't know. Grace, whatever you do, you mustn't tell anyone about this."

"About what?"

"Please just don't. You can't," Agnes begged. "Nothing's the matter now anyway. He's only had a bad night, and that's the end of it. He'll be fine after some sleep, I'm sure. Promise me you won't tell anyone, Grace, especially Dr. McCabe."

"But what happened?"

"He locked himself in his closet last night," said Agnes. "And it terrified him. I don't know why."

"But that would only be natural," Grace replied. "You know what some of those camps were like. He was probably shut up in a box for hours or days. I'm sure he would be very disturbed by small spaces."

"Oh, no," Agnes murmured, dropping her head into her hands.

"I didn't mean to upset you, Miss Starbuck," the young nurse said quickly. "But I was a nurse's aide during the war, and I discovered that such things did happen."

"No, it's fine," Agnes returned, waving her hand. "It's just so wicked. I can't bear to think of what he must have gone through. You won't tell the doctor about last night, will you?"

"No. It's only something to be careful of, that's all. It's perfectly normal, though. It's not, well—"

"Yes, I know," Agnes interjected. "Thank you."

"Grace, why did you move to Cot's Haven?" Eva asked after lunch one day.

Grace looked up from washing dishes.

"Whatever made you think of that?" she said.

Eva shrugged.

"Well, I can think of two reasons," the nurse replied, cocking her head meditatively. "The first would be Carter."

"Who's that?"

"The new postman."

"Oh, Carter Tankard!" Eva smiled. "He used to go fishing with Mr. York and my father. There was something about him in the paper last week. Isn't he engaged to someone?"

"Yes," said Grace, "me."

"You?"

"Indeed!"

"Why, congratulations! He's a very nice fellow," Eva declared.

"I think so, too," Grace blushed.

"When are you getting married?"

"In the spring, we hope."

"Will you stop working then?" Eva pressed.

"Oh, I see what you're getting at. I don't think so, not for a few years."

"Wonderful!" Eva grinned. "What's the other reason?"

"The other reason," Grace said, sitting down at the table, "is my father."

"Does he live here, too?"

"No," Grace shook her head. "My father died in a prison camp during the war. Many, many men died in that camp. In fact, as far as everyone knows, only five prisoners ever escaped. There was an American named Euston, a boy named Short, a Farnham, a Johnston, and a sergeant named Starbuck."

Eva's mouth dropped.

"Most of these soldiers were taken to hospitals far away from here, so I never saw them," Grace said. "But your father was brought to St. Anne's. I don't think that was an accident, just as I don't think it was an accident that a year ago I became engaged to a man who lives only a few miles from this house. Eva, I'll never see my father again in this life, but every day I look at Mr. Starbuck and think, *If I can't have my father, then I'll make sure someone else can have theirs as long as possible.*"

"I wish you could stay with us forever," Eva said quietly.

"I wish I could, too," Grace smiled. "But don't worry. I shan't be leaving for a long time."

Chapter 9

A gloomy wet December had settled in that year, dragging along with it an equally dismal prediction for Christmas. While the Starbucks had never been rich, this was a challenging year even by their standards. Ulysses' military compensations were meager and unable to cover both the hospital bills and Grace's small salary. Agnes's position of secretary to Mr. Surrey provided nominal pay at best.

Even so, Agnes and Eva were trying to make the best of the hard time. After all, if they could not buy many things, they could at least make them. As Christmas approached, each spent many secret moments knitting or baking or gluing gifts while the other was away or asleep.

It was just one of these nights while Agnes slept that Eva chose to stay up and crochet a flowered doily for the back of her aunt's favorite chair. So absorbed was she in her work that she was surprised to hear the hall clock strike one. With a sigh, the girl stretched out her cramped fingers and was admiring her work when she heard footsteps in the hall. Frantically, she shoved the doily into a basket, turned off her lamp, and hopped as noiselessly as possible into bed.

The door flew open.

"Eva."

Eva pretended to sleep.

"Eva, this is important."

"Mmm, what is it, Aunty?" Eva yawned.

"Is your father in here?"

The girl shot up in bed.

"What do you mean?"

"He's not in his room," Agnes replied, her voice tight and tense.

"Have you checked his closet?" Eva asked, pushing off her bed covers.

"Of course! That's the first place I looked. Now don't be alarmed, because I haven't searched everywhere yet. I was just starting with the bedrooms, that's all."

"Oh, Aunty, what if something terrible has happened?"

"What if you help me?" Agnes replied. "I'm off to the kitchen and back garden. You look in the sitting room for a start. And whatever you do, don't shout his name. He can hear you perfectly well if you speak plainly. I don't want the neighbors to hear you and think something's wrong."

Obediently, Eva hurried to the sitting room where she peered behind furniture and into corners and called as loudly as she dared. But Ulysses was not in the sitting room, or the hall closet, or in the front garden. Near the front door, Eva met her aunt again and discovered that her search was also fruitless.

"What are we going to do?" Eva moaned, sniffling.

"Shh! Now stop it," Agnes ordered. "Pull yourself together, child."

"But he's gone!" Eva persisted. "Where could he go? Why would he leave? We've got to call the Yorks or the police!"

"We'll do no such thing!" Agnes growled. "We will start the search over again. We will keep our heads and look everywhere

81

twice. And when you've looked in a room, I'll go in and look into it myself, and so forth. Do you understand, Eva? We shall keep our heads!"

"Oh, he's really gone!" Eva burbled.

"Stop it!" Agnes commanded, grabbing Eva's shoulders and shaking her firmly. "Now go begin with your room while I look in your father's."

Still whimpering, Eva whirled around and raced down the hall to her room. The place appeared just as empty as it had been twenty minutes ago. It made no sense that she was searching for her father's towering figure in a tiny room she had been in moments before, but Eva was going to search anyway.

Wiping her eyes with her sleeve, she bent down and looked under the skirt of her bed.

"Daddy!" she called into the piles of old books, unmatched shoes, broken pencils, and general rubbish. "He's not here!"

"You haven't finished looking!" Agnes yelled, forgetting to be quiet.

"But he can't be here," Eva groaned to herself. "He just can't!"

But back she went to her closet and gazed inside. There was nothing but dresses, sweaters, and boxes without end.

No one could hide in there.

"Aunty," she started to shout, turning from her closet in disgust and disappointment, "he's not—"

Her next word was sucked back into her with a gasp. For there, sitting on the edge of her bed, looking about like a lost child, was her father.

"Daddy!" she exclaimed, and, without even thinking, she dashed to his side and wrapped her arms around his neck.

That precious moment was not to last long. Ulysses promptly peeled the girl away and stood up.

"Aunty!" Eva shouted. "I've found him!"

"Where?" cried Agnes, sprinting into the room.

"Here!" Eva said. "He must have been following us the whole time!"

After Agnes led her brother back to his bed, she returned to Eva's room.

"Well," she said, "I told you we mustn't lose our heads. Anyway, tomorrow is Saturday, so I'm off for a good long sleep. Good night!"

"Night, Aunty," Eva smiled, snuggling under her blankets.

About an hour later, Eva was awakened by her door creaking open. Blinking, she saw her father's silhouette standing black against the dimly lit hall.

"Daddy?"

The figure turned and vanished. Hastily, Eva crawled out of bed and looked into the hall. Just in time, she spotted her father disappearing into his room. She stayed there until she heard his bed creak; then, with a sigh, she returned to her own.

∾

"What do you think about Christmas?" Harold asked as he walked Eva home from the train station Tuesday afternoon.

"I doubt it," she said, pushing her cycle along.

"Well, you should ask her, at least," he reasoned. "After all, lots of people go to services on Christmas who don't usually. And she'd be going so your dad could, too."

"Harold, Aunty hasn't gone to a church in my life," Eva said. "I don't see why she shouldn't skip this Christmas along with all the others."

"Well, we could take you and your father," Harold suggested.

"Oh, no," Eva shook her head. "Aunty wouldn't have that at

all. She'd be furious. And anyway, I wouldn't want you to go to all that trouble."

"What trouble could there be? All he does is sit quietly, doesn't he?"

"Mostly," Eva muttered.

"Well, that's the perfect thing for church, you know. Why, I was far more trouble than that five years ago," Harold chuckled. "And anyway, Dad and Mr. Starbuck were real mates, they were. Dad wouldn't think it a bit of trouble if we took him along. He talks about him a lot, you know, wondering how he's doing and all. Did you know, every time Dad or Mum telephones to see about dropping by, your aunt has an excuse?"

"What do you mean?" Eva asked, stopping.

"Oh, I don't mean it's not a real excuse," Harold corrected himself. "It's just that your dad's always sleeping or not feeling well, or everyone's busy with this or that."

"Really," Eva mumbled.

"Well, anyway, here we are!" said Harold. "And here's your aunt. Hallo, Miss Starbuck!" he greeted, taking off his cap. "How are you this afternoon?"

"Fine, thank you," Agnes said, coming down the steps to the walk.

She looked worried and agitated about something, but only Eva noticed this.

"What about Christmas at Cotter's Church, Miss Starbuck?" Harold asked very politely. "We'd love to have you join us."

Agnes's face tinged just a little red.

"Thank you, no," she said stiffly. "Eva, you'd better come in now. It's too cold. Goodbye, Harold."

Harold, characteristic to his usual open-faced nature, hardly hid his surprise at this cold brush off; but he still gave the ladies a rustic bow and walked off civilly.

"Aunty," Eva said, following Agnes into the house. "Why can't the Yorks come see us these days?"

"If you must know, you father needs his rest," her aunt replied, starting off down the hall. "That's an end of it."

"Wait, why are you home this early?" Eva asked, struck by the strange situation.

"Grace called me," Agnes said, turning to Eva.

The color drained from Eva's face.

"What happened, Aunty?"

"We didn't want to say anything to you yesterday, because there was no reason to upset you," Agnes explained; "but now you'll find out anyway, so I shall tell you. Your father has been unwell. He spent most of yesterday and all last night trying to get out of the house."

"But Aunty, he can't even get a door open," Eva observed.

"No, but he's been quite upset and won't eat or sleep. And now he's running a fever. That's why Grace called me."

"What did the doctor say?"

"He hasn't been here."

"Why not?"

"Because he's not needed, Eva," Agnes returned sharply. "We can manage this without his help. Don't you want your father to remember things?"

"You know I do!"

"Well, Dr. McCabe won't help him do that. He'd give him a sedative or worse, and Ulysses would forget to even try and remember anything. I'm sure we'll make much more progress if we take care of him ourselves. And don't tell anybody about this, Eva, because everything anyone says in Cot's Haven comes round to the doctor eventually. If he got the least hint that something was amiss, he'd meddle for certain."

"Yes, Aunty."

"Not even the Yorks," Agnes emphasized.

"No one," Eva replied.

"Now, don't worry," Agnes said, giving her niece's arm an encouraging squeeze. "Your father will be all right again soon."

But he was not. All that week, Ulysses paced about, shoving against doors and windows, prying at panels in the walls, trying to get out of that house with a dogged desperation that bordered on insanity. At first, his obsession would occur sporadically, with periods of fitful rest in between; but by the end of the week, the problem had become constant. He was getting no sleep, eating and drinking almost nothing, and persistently being plagued by a dull fever.

Something would have to break soon, or the obsession would break him.

"Miss Starbuck, tomorrow I'm calling the doctor," Grace said that Saturday night after she had given up her weekend to look after Ulysses.

"What?" Agnes replied, nearly dropping the basket of groceries she had brought in.

"I should have telephoned him a week ago," Grace continued. "Miss Starbuck, your brother needs help."

"Not from any doctors!"

"You can't help him, Agnes," Grace said. "I can't help him. How long do you think he can go on this way? How long can you go on like this? Look at you: you haven't gotten any more sleep than he has. You're worried sick, and so is Eva."

"If you feel your position is too difficult," Agnes seethed, clenching her basket, "you can leave any time you wish, Miss Watkins."

"I'm not thinking about me!" Grace retorted, abandoning her usual sweet, unruffled manner. "I'm thinking about Mr.

Starbuck and you and Eva. I'm thinking about all of you! Miss Starbuck, this must stop!"

"Maybe you can't go on this way," Agnes replied angrily. "And in that case, you can give notice as soon as you like. Don't worry, I'll give you a nice reference and forget about this conversation."

"Can't you understand?" Grace cried. "I don't want to leave!"

During this heated argument, Eva sat in her room, staring blankly at a single page from *The Wind in the Willows*. She could hear the voices rising and falling in the kitchen. This was the third dispute between her aunt and Grace in the past two days, and the girl could guess where it would end. Grace would agree to wait one more day, and Agnes would agree not to discharge her.

While those two might go on this way indefinitely, Eva knew her father could not. Every day and every night she had prayed that God would heal him of this mad fixation, but Ulysses was only getting worse.

"You can't help him!" Grace shouted from across the house.

"But *You* can," Eva whispered, gazing up at the ceiling. "Why won't You?"

As the quarrel in the kitchen subsided to a murmur, Eva sat on her bed a moment longer. Then she shut her book with a bang and headed for her father's room. Pushing the door open, she peeped in, expecting to see Ulysses knocking bric-a-brac off the walls and shoving against the paneling. But instead, he was on the floor, crumpled beside the bed. From where Eva stood, she could see that his dark-rimmed eyes were half-open. In his lap lay his hands, with the nails on his remaining fingers broken and bleeding from scratching at the walls. He looked utterly spent.

"Daddy, why don't you just go to sleep?"

Even as the girl spoke, Ulysses stirred, staggered to his feet, and dragged himself to the window to try and push it open.

Eva wanted so badly to take him back to the floor, but

she knew he would only get up again. Angry and afraid, she returned to her room and slammed the door behind her. Then she hurriedly threw herself into her bed and turned her reading lamp out. After all, tears were so much easier to hide in the dark.

Chapter 10

"It's Friday the twenty-first! Christmas Eve's in three days!" the large and ruddy Ronald Surrey boomed, poking his head into his outer office at the factory.

"So it is!" Agnes smiled, looking up from her typewriter.

"Well, get on with you, then," Mr. Surrey grinned. "I'm shutting down the factory early today."

"Oh, well if you need me to stay and finish these letters, I will," Agnes said hastily.

"No, no, no, you'll be paid for the whole day," the man shook his head with a laugh. "I'm giving you a ten-minute head start before I release the monkeys. Get on, then!"

Agnes stepped out of the building five minutes later. Eager to get ahead of the crowd, she trotted to the bicycle racks.

Her cycle was not where she had left it. Grumbling about misplacing it and dismissing the wild idea that someone had stolen the tired old thing, Agnes began to walk up and down the rows of cycles.

"Ah, Miss Starbuck?" said a voice.

Agnes turned and found herself staring up at Major Arnold's fuzzy gray moustache and sky-blue eyes.

"Oh!" she exclaimed. "Major!"

"Yes, miss," he returned, touching his cap.

"We haven't seen you in some time, sir. What brings you back to Cot's Haven?"

"Well," he said deliberately, folding his hands behind his back, "something rather important, I believe. I have tried to contact you for the past two days, but without success. I'm afraid your nurse may have forgotten to give you my messages."

"I am sorry," Agnes replied. "Things have been rather busy lately."

"I apologize if this is an inconvenient time, our dropping in without any notice like this; but it couldn't wait a day longer."

"Dropping in?"

"Yes, may we drive you home?"

"We?"

"Miss Starbuck, I've found someone who knew your brother quite well. He is an American named Corporal Euston. He was imprisoned in Das Grab with your brother."

"I'm very sorry for him," Agnes answered sincerely. "But I don't understand what brings you both here."

"We think I can help the sergeant."

Looking behind the major, Agnes saw a short, dark-haired man approaching. He was about thirty-five, with hazel eyes, a bronzed complexion, and a smiling face.

"This is Corporal Morton Euston," the major said as the man walked up. "Corporal, this is Miss Starbuck."

"Mr. Mort Euston these days," the man corrected good-naturedly, warmly grasping the hand Agnes offered him. "It's a real pleasure, ma'am."

Agnes could not help noticing that two fingers on his right hand were missing. But barring this sad absence and a few oddly shaped scars on his face, Euston looked remarkably well considering his imprisonment.

Just then the factory whistle peeled off like a train, and a stream of employees started to flow into the car park.

"Perhaps we'd better talk on the way to my vehicle," the major suggested, taking Agnes's arm.

"My bicycle is here somewhere," Agnes said, glancing behind them as they started off.

"I took the liberty of putting it in my car," Arnold replied frankly, seemingly unaware of the boldness of the deed. "It's only a short walk. You will recall that when we last met, I explained that the Army had special cause investigate certain events that took place in Das Grab. That investigation is still in progress."

"I don't know what information you and Mr. Euston think you can get from my brother," Agnes remarked. "He can't tell you anything. He can't even speak."

"But we're not here for that, ma'am," said Euston, walking alongside the two.

"Miss Starbuck," Arnold continued, pausing as they reached his vehicle and looking at her seriously, "I know that you don't have the highest opinion of me or the British Army. You have good reasons. But despite what you may think, I haven't brought Euston with me on military business. I've brought him here because I want to help your brother.

"In the process of my investigation, I met Euston and discovered that his relationship to your brother was more than the usual comradery that develops when men live together in appalling circumstances. He wasn't a man in another barracks or across the compound in Das Grab. He spent most of his imprisonment in the same barracks as your brother and knew him extremely well.

"Now, I don't pretend to be a doctor, but I have talked to specialists who have told me of cases in which men with damaged minds have regained some part of themselves by being exposed to very familiar people and places."

"Ulysses has been exposed to those things, Major," Agnes commented. "He has been in his home with his family for months."

"Meaning no disrespect," Euston broke in, "but I believe the last time he saw you was in '39. I was sleeping in the bunk above him in Das Grab until just last year. Maybe he can't remember you yet, because you're too far away. Maybe first he needs to remember someone like me, who's closer to where he is now, before he can remember you."

Agnes looked from one man to the other. She couldn't think of what to say. Inside she felt that someone had come along, taken her forgotten hope from a dark shelf, and blown the dust off it. And the feeling alarmed her.

"Why are you doing this for us?" she finally asked.

"Ma'am," Euston replied, "your brother was the only thing that kept me alive in that camp. All I had was guts, but he had hope. And his hope and courage is what kept a lot of us going for so long. In Das Grab I'd have died for him if I could've. I never got the chance. But if I can do anything for him before I go back home to the States, I'll do it in a heartbeat."

"Do you really think this could work?" Agnes asked, turning to the major.

"I think," said the officer, opening the passenger door, "that for a man like Starbuck, it is certainly worth trying."

The arrival of Major Arnold and Morton Euston was so unexpected that at first Agnes did not have time to think. There was no time to think about the surprise of coming home with the gentlemen, no time to consider the untidy condition of her house, and no time to worry over the present condition of her brother. But, as Arnold was easing his lumbering black vehicle into the street, everything hit Agnes at once.

"Wait," she said, her eyes widening. "You said you couldn't delay another day."

"Yes, we did," the major asserted.

"It must be today, this very afternoon? You couldn't possibly make it tomorrow or the next?"

"Why, no," Arnold returned, glancing in her direction. "The corporal is leaving for the states tomorrow morning."

"I could stay later if I'm needed," Euston offered from the rear seat.

"No, I wouldn't ask you to do that," Agnes said, her heart sinking.

"Is something wrong?" Arnold questioned.

Agnes stared ahead at the houses flitting by one by one. They would be in front of the Starbuck home in less than twenty minutes.

"Miss Starbuck?"

Agnes was being torn apart inside.

"Well," she said at last, "I was wondering what good there would be in Mr. Euston having one visit, or even a few visits, and then leaving for America and not coming back. That doesn't give my brother long to remember anything."

"Regrettably so," acknowledged the major. "However, I feel the chance is worth taking. It certainly cannot hurt him, and it might just help. Don't you think?"

Agnes could only nod in reply.

Soon Arnold was driving up to the curb in front of the house. Euston jumped out of the vehicle and opened the door for Agnes.

Stepping out, Agnes tested her weak legs on the firm stones in the walkway. In a haze, she led the men up the steps, ushered them inside, and closed the door. The soft *thunk* of the wood against the frame had a dull sense of finality to Agnes's ears.

"Is that you, Aunty?" Eva's voice called from the sitting room.

"Yes," she replied, closing her eyes a second. "There's some gentlemen here, too."

Eva stepped into the hall.

"It's Major Arnold!" she said, looking rather confused.

"This," Agnes said, addressing Euston, "is my niece Eva. Eva, this is Mr. Euston. He knew your father during the war."

"It's very nice to meet you," Eva replied, shaking the hand extended to her and looking expectantly at her aunt.

"Where is your father?" Agnes inquired.

"On the sofa," said Eva, trying to read the strange expression on her aunt's face.

Agnes was about to suggest that the gentlemen go to the kitchen for a cup of tea, but Mr. Euston, upon hearing where his old sergeant was, walked right into the sitting room before Agnes could stop him.

As Agnes knew and feared, Ulysses was, quite bluntly, a wreck. Sleepless nights, rejected meals, and relentless obsession had siphoned every semblance of wellness clean out of him. He was haggard, drooping, and withered like some weary ancient—the ghostly remnants of a man.

Agnes felt ill. She looked at Major Arnold and read the surprise on his face. He glanced in her direction, but she could not look him in the eye. In contrast, Morton Euston did not act shocked in the least degree. Composedly, he picked up a nearby stool, set it before Ulysses, and sat down facing him.

"Hey, Sergeant," the man said.

"He can't hear you," Eva piped up.

Euston smiled at Eva, but he promptly turned back to her father. For a few moments, it was silent in that room. Euston stared at Ulysses. The others stood motionless, watching the American intently.

"Sergeant," he said at length, "it's Mort Euston."

But Ulysses did not respond. Abruptly, Euston leaned forward, seized Ulysses' face, and brought it upward.

"Hey," he commanded, "look at me!"

Agnes or Eva might have stepped in to pull Euston away, but before they could, something shocking occurred. Gradually, Ulysses' eyes rolled upward, traveling up the other man's shirt, until they locked with Euston's eyes.

Instantly, it seemed as if the sun had sprung from behind a blanket of storm clouds. His eyes widening, Ulysses sucked in a mouthful of air through cracked lips and feebly lifted a hand to touch the other man. But then, as rapidly as it had emerged, the daylight vanished. His face darkened, his eyes lost their light, and his upraised head sank downward. And once again, Ulysses Starbuck was not at home.

No one spoke for a while. At length, Agnes cleared her throat.

"Thank you for trying," she said, still looking at her brother. "I'd rather you not try again just now."

"Sure, no problem," Euston answered. "If I could get a later boat, I could try another time."

"No," Agnes said, managing a feeble smile, "thank you very much. This has been a great strain on him, and I shouldn't risk it so soon."

"Perhaps we had better leave, now," the major suggested.

"Yeah, guess so," said Euston, noticing the wooden look on Agnes's face and the distress in Eva's eyes. "It was real nice meeting you all. I wish you the best of luck. And if you ever think I can help, you can write me at this address."

"Thank you so much," Agnes restated, rousing herself in time to take the notecard Euston handed her. "Let me show you to the door."

When Agnes came back, Eva was waiting for her in a chair near the fire.

"They've gone," Agnes sighed, dropping into her own chair.

"I saw him," Eva murmured. "I saw Daddy just for a second, there at the end."

"So did I," Agnes returned. "And I wish to God I had not seen that."

The encounter with Euston was just enough to tip Ulysses over the brink. By Christmas Eve, he was delirious with fever.

"Can we please call the doctor, now?" Eva asked that morning.

"Yes," Agnes yielded, watching miserably as her brother groaned and shivered in his bed. "I'll do it at once."

Dr. McCabe arrived within an hour, wearing a festive red tie and green waistcoat. His attire badly fitted the mood of that house.

"Who is Selkirk?" he asked, coming into the kitchen from Ulysses' room.

"Selkirk?" Agnes echoed, pausing her potato slicing.

"Yes."

"I don't know anyone by that name."

"Well, Starbuck does," the doctor said, plopping into a kitchen chair and setting his bag on the table. "That's the only word he's spoken since I arrived."

"Spoken! He hasn't said anything since Patrick found him!"

"Well, don't let it bring your hopes up too high," McCabe returned bluntly, snatching a potato peeling from the table and popping it into his mouth. "He was raving. The name may have no more meaning to him that it does to you or I."

"Yes, but he spoke!"

"Agnes, that means very little," the doctor replied brusquely. "Your brother is in ruins, and he has been for some time. You should have called for me long before today. His mental state is poor enough, but when you let him dissipate physically—why didn't you tell me?"

"I didn't think you could help."

"That's not true and you know it."

"Then I was confident that, between Grace and I, we could handle the situation," Agnes contended.

"She could hardly do more than you at a certain point, Agnes, as long as you were keeping her from obtaining my aid."

"Did she tell you that?" Agnes asked, raising an eyebrow.

"No, I guessed it," McCabe replied. "You do me a great discredit. I'm not so easy to fool as some people in this village may think. It's doctors that are lied to the most, you know. We've had a great deal of practice learning how to read closed books."

"That is neither here nor there," Agnes concluded crossly. "What I want to know is how my brother is now."

"Keep ice on him, let him rest, and get him to drink as much as possible," said the doctor. "His fever's gone down, but it will likely go up again. There is a long night ahead. Are you prepared to stay up with him again?"

"Again?"

"Yes, again, Agnes. You're forgetting I'm not a fool, although I must admit any child could guess from your appearance how many hours of sleep you've missed and how much weight you've lost."

"He's my brother, doctor," Agnes said. "I'll miss as many hours as I like."

"Just so you know it will catch up with you," McCabe said, rising. "The fiddler isn't cheap."

"I'm willing to pay for it. Good morning, doctor."

"You know," the man said, pausing in the kitchen doorway, "you don't have to do this to yourself. And, I might add, you don't have to do this to Eva. There are people that will take him. There's an excellent institution in Portsmouth."

"My brother," Agnes responded icily, "is never going to one of those places."

"I know how you feel, Agnes. And I know why. But the time may come again when you don't have a choice."

"I'll decide that."

"Well, at any rate, I'll be back Thursday," McCabe announced, putting on his hat. "I do wish you all a Happy Christmas. And I believe it's Ulysses' birthday tomorrow?"

Agnes looked up at the ceiling and bit her lip.

"You'll not take it in jest if I wish him a fair one," McCabe said, "as empty as that sounds. Good night."

When Eva awoke early the next morning, the house was quiet. It must have been early indeed, for, excluding the trills of a few winter songbirds, the street outside was equally still. Not even the Christmas church bells had begun to ring.

Ah yes, Christmas. It did not feel like a Christmas to Eva. She didn't want it to be Christmas—not yet, not until the dark, long nightmare in that house was over. In the sitting room there were three lumpy stockings sagging above a cold hearth, but Eva had no desire to look into them.

It was odd. Several years ago, Eva would awaken before sunrise on Christmas, go bounding and singing into her father's bedroom, and pester him to get up. The answer was always, "No, sweetheart, not until dawn." So, the child would crawl into her father's bed and lie there with her head on his chest, listening to his steady heartbeat and peering eagerly out the window for the arrival of the sun.

Today she was no more tired than she had been so many years ago, but that childlike eagerness was now gone. Sluggishly, the girl shuffled to the kitchen.

It was empty, and cold. Her aunt must not have been up yet. A trip to Agnes's room confirmed this notion: Eva found her snoring under a thick mound of covers. Stepping into the hall, the girl wondered what to do next. She gazed despairingly down the darkly paneled, lonely corridor and hated it. She hated all those lonely rooms and hated that house.

Except her father's room. Somehow today it did not feel as lonesome as the rest of the house. Soon she found her feet wandering in that direction and her hands pushing his door open.

Her father was lying in bed, his shirt and hair still damp from the fever that had broken a few hours before. Sitting down in the same chair she had struck her head on earlier that month, Eva rested her chin in her palm and gazed at her father.

It had been a while since Eva really looked at Ulysses. When he was awake, he was so unbearably different. But when he was asleep, he almost seemed like his old self. That sad, troubled expression was smoothed out; the dull, unseeing eyes were closed; and the crumpled figure was stretched and relaxed. It might have been Christmas morning seven years ago, and Eva might be there to be held by her father and wait for the dawn.

"Please, God," Eva prayed, "If you just give him back, I'll never ask You for anything ever again. I'd give up anything for that! Please, please, I miss him so much!"

And then, for the first time in six years, Eva leaned forward, gently parted her father's hair, and kissed his angel mark.

That was her birthday present to him. She would not kiss her father again for a long time.

Chapter 11

During her father's recent health crisis, Eva had almost forgotten about Roger Wyatt. When she did stop to think of it, bothering herself about Roger seemed rather stupid. He was probably a dull sort or an insufferable fop, and even if he happened to a nice boy, he certainly couldn't be expected to care particularly about her.

Mandy was not of the same opinion. In that little blonde bob of hers resided an exceptional imagination, a measure of emotional inconsistency, and a cosmic stock of memories from a tidy library of romance novels. All these energies she was more than willing to propel toward the first striking lad she was introduced to.

Although Mandy had not yet been introduced to Roger Wyatt, that was a little problem she was working on.

"You're balmy!" Eva cried as she and Mandy walked ahead of several other navy-clad, straw-hatted Southdale girls going to the train station.

"I am not, Eva!" Mandy maintained. "It's all perfectly reasonable, and you don't have to do hardly a thing."

"Except try and run you down with my bicycle!" Eva scoffed.

"Oh, that's the easiest part of the whole plan!" Mandy said with a carefree twist of her hat.

"I didn't say it would be hard," Eva corrected. "I just don't happen to enjoy killing my friends, that's all."

"But you won't!" Mandy objected. "Roger Wyatt will be there to save me! Oh, it will be so dreamy, Eva, just like it was in *Rosy Wilson's First Love*. And you'll get to meet him, too."

"I couldn't care less."

"You didn't think so last month," Mandy remarked. "You thought he was delicious!"

"Well, he's not anymore. I won't do it, Mandy, and that's that. Even if I did think he was good-looking, I wouldn't run anyone down for him."

"Oh, please, Eva!" Mandy whined. "No one else will do it. I've asked everyone in our form! I need someone to help me!"

"What kind of help do you need, Mandy dear?"

"Priscilla!" Mandy yipped as the other girl quickened her pace to keep in step with the two friends.

"I thought I heard you say you needed help," Priscilla smiled. "You sounded so very desperate. Is there something I can do?"

"I doubt it," Eva mumbled.

"What do you think of Roger Wyatt?" asked Mandy.

Priscilla's face flushed for a fraction of an instant, but when she replied her voice was as calm and cool as ever.

"Oh," she shrugged, catching some of her hair to twirl, "he's all right."

"I've got a scheme to meet him," Mandy explained eagerly, "and all I need is someone to ride a bicycle near his house."

"Ha!" Eva snorted.

"If you'll help me, Priscilla, you and I could both meet him!"

"But Mandy darling, wouldn't it be simpler if I introduced you to him?" Priscilla suggested.

"You know him?"

"We've met."

"And you'd take me to meet him?"

"Of course, dear!"

"Oh, how lucky!" Mandy squealed rapturously. "Would you take Eva, too?"

"Certainly, if she wants to come," said Priscilla, eying the other girl.

"I couldn't care less," Eva affirmed.

"What a shame," Priscilla replied in a tone that was supposed to sound sad. "Well, Mandy, I think we can do well enough by ourselves. When we get to Cot's Haven, why don't you and I have tea at Bordeaux's first?"

"Bordeaux's!"

"Certainly! And then I can take you to meet him at the grocers where he works."

"Isn't the grocers a little common for you?" Eva questioned, glaring at Priscilla.

"Oh, I'd do anything for Mandy," Priscilla cooed. "She's such a dear girl!"

When the train arrived at Cot's Haven, Priscilla and her admiring new companion went giggling off to Bordeaux's Café, leaving Eva alone with an errand to run. Growling to herself like an injured animal, Eva rode down the street to the local garage where Mandy's older brother Desmond was apprenticed. Speedily she told him to tell his twin Ira to tell their mother (and to probably not tell their father) that Mandy was off with the Duff's youngest daughter and would be home before dark. After leaving Desmond in a state of surprise, Eva pedaled angrily for home.

There really was nothing to be angry about. After all, as Eva herself had mentioned, she "couldn't care less" to meet that Wyatt fellow. But the thought of one of her best friends following that prig Priscilla Duff around like a slave boiled her blood. And the more she thought about it, the more her blood boiled; and the more her blood boiled, the faster she cycled; and the faster she cycled, the less attention she paid to the road before her.

Heaven only knows what her blood pressure was when she got to her street. She didn't even know she had just turned into her neighborhood until she happened to look up.

Scrrreeeeecchh! Eva slammed on her break only just in time.

"Oh, my goodness, I'm so sorry!" she squeaked.

"That's all right!" the boy in front of her smiled, revealing those sinfully white teeth.

"Did I hurt you?"

"Oh, no," he replied, looking down at his leg. "I think you missed me by about an inch."

"I'm really sorry," Eva emphasized, still trembling from the shock.

"And I'm really all right," the boy laughed.

"You're sure?"

"Positive."

"Oh, good," Eva breathed. "Hallo," she added. "You're Roger Wyatt."

"Yes, and I believe you're my neighbor."

"Oh," Eva said, reddening at her recollection of the girls' vigil by the window the previous month. "Yes."

"Well, since you know my name, why don't you tell me yours," he grinned.

"Eva—Starbuck," she stammered, trying to get her mind off all that beautifully blonde hair.

"Pleasure. I say, you still look rather shaken. May I walk you to your house?"

The words *of course* were forming in Eva's mouth. But then she imagined the jokes Harold would create if he happened to see her walking down the street with this boy.

"Maybe another time," she said. "I've got to cycle home as quickly as possible, or someone will worry about me. I'm rather late as it is."

"Well then, be careful and don't hit anyone!" Roger said with a wink.

When Eva reached the Starbuck cottage, a thought struck her.

"'Maybe another time'?" she restated. "I thought I couldn't care less! Eva Starbuck, what on earth were you thinking?"

~๑

"Two families in as many months," said Barney Mulchin, owner and proprietor of Mulchin's Pub. "First those Wyatt folks and now—what's their names?"

"Abernathy," Patrick York replied after a drink from his mug.

"Scots," rumbled Clint Fraser from the other end of the bar.

"Yes, well, it just proves what I always say," Barney proceeded. "Things happen in stages in this village. It never rains but it pours."

"I hope it don't pour more outsiders," Fraser complained. "Who needs 'em?"

"I do, for one thing," Barney pointed out. "I've got a business to run, and so do the other merchants in Cot's Haven. Anyway, there's nothing wrong with a few new faces. It's good for the village, mixing up stagnant water so to speak."

"Well, those Wyatts are all right," said Fraser, "but I'll wager that Scotsman and his wife are trouble."

"I met Abernathy only this morning," Mr. York said, "and he seems like a decent sort. What've you got against them, anyway, Fraser?"

"They're Scots," the sailor shrugged, "and Scots with the sourest faces I ever did see."

"Anyone'd have a sour face after the first time he met

you, Fraser," Barney chuckled. "And wasn't your granddad a Scotsman?"

"Well, the point is—by Jove, speak o' the devil!" Fraser broke off in an urgent whisper, jabbing his thumb in the direction of the door.

As he was speaking, a tall, thin, sallow-faced gentleman entered Mulchin's Pub. His quick, firm gait put his age at about fifty years, but the lines on his face and the graveness of his features suggested he was much older. He stepped swiftly up to the bar and slapped some coins onto the counter.

"Whisky, sir," he said in a crisp Scottish accent.

"Well, hallo, Abernathy!" Patrick York addressed the man, taking his drink and moving a couple stools closer to him.

Mr. Abernathy squinted down at him like a man used to wearing glasses.

"Patrick York," Mr. York said. "We met this morning at the post office."

"Ah, York!" Abernathy exclaimed. "Pleasure t' see ye again. Ye'll forgive me, I've met so many people this past week."

"Not at all. How does our little village strike you?"

"Small and dirty," Clint Fraser inserted, glowering at the stranger from over his mug.

"Pat didn't ask Abernathy how *you* strike him," Barney said, setting down the man's whisky and shooting Fraser a scowl.

"It is small," Abernathy admitted, disregarding Fraser's stares. "My wife and I are used t' the city, ye understand. But I think it's very quaint, and we shall like it here also."

"Oh, where are you from?" Barney asked.

"Edinburgh."

Barney whistled and looked impressed.

"Whereabouts in Edinburgh?" Clint queried.

"It's no' easy t' describe unless ye've been there," Abernathy said, gulping down his whisky and rising. "I must be leaving no', if ye'll excuse me, gentlemen."

Patrick and the bartender toasted the man's health, but Fraser maintained a cold silence as the man departed.

"Edinburgh," he grunted a moment later. "Bah!"

"What's wrong with that?" Barney inquired.

"D'you here how he said it? 'Edinburg' he said, like a burg."

"I suppose he made a mistake," Patrick offered.

"D'you ever hear a Scot mispronounce Edinburgh?"

"Yes, just now," Patrick replied.

"That's no Scot."

"Fraser," Barney said sternly, "if you'd keep your trap shut and use your brains more often, you wouldn't make such a fool of yourself. If the man says he's a Scot from Edinburgh, there's no reason you shouldn't believe him until you've *got* a reason, see?"

"Well, I'd say I have!"

"I've had about all I can take from you this evening," Barney rumbled. "Why don't you go home to bed and rest your mouth."

Fraser's mouth fell open a second, but nothing came out of it. Then he whirled about, popped off his stool like a cork out of a bottle, and scuttled out of the building without a word of farewell.

"You've made the old fellow sore," Patrick said.

"Well, he needed it," Barney complained. "Every single day I listen to him weaving the most crackbrained tales you ever heard. It's enough to drive a man batty. Abernathy not a Scotsman— that's ridiculous!"

"It was rather absurd," Patrick affirmed.

"I'll eat this glass here if there's ever a shred of truth in what Clint Fraser says," Barney huffed. "He hasn't been right in thirty years."

While the worthy bartender and Mr. York were discussing

the old sailor's veracity in the pub, Fraser himself was slouching down the darkening street on his way home.

"Rest my mouth," Fraser grumbled. "That Barney ought to rest his own mouth, he should. Bah!"

He hadn't gone far down the street when he spied the slim form of Mr. Abernathy strolling hurriedly ahead of him in the fading light.

"Well," Fraser huffed, picking up his own pace, "Barney calls me a fool, does he? We'll just see about this."

And with that, the old sailor started after the sour-faced Scotsman, until eventually the figures of both men melted away into the night.

Chapter 12

It was finally spring, and Grace Watkins was half out of her mind with joy. May was just around the corner, and May 1946 meant marriage for Miss Watkins.

Now, Grace had always been a sensible young woman. Perhaps the fact that her head had been so tightly screwed on all her life was why it abruptly jarred loose that spring. In truth, the young nurse was having a difficult time paying attention to anything besides Carter Tankard. While preparing breakfast or folding laundry for her patient, all she could think of was how nice it would be to do those wifely tasks for Carter. If she walked with Ulysses in the garden, she spent the time mentally rehearsing the right moment her uncle Russell should lead her down the aisle.

The worst thing about it was that she was so used to being sensible that she hardly noticed this change in herself. And so, as the days and weeks passed, Grace grew more and more distant from her life and duties in the Starbuck home.

She was not the only one.

"Mandy, can you keep a secret?" Eva asked one day when her friend had dropped by to enjoy the strip of beachfront behind the house.

"To my dying breath!" Mandy cried, scooting her beach chair closer to Eva's.

"I think my aunt's in love."

"Your aunt!" Mandy breathed, clapping her hand to her mouth. "But she's so—so—"

"Cold? Reserved? Stern?" Eva finished. "It's not that I don't love her dearly, you understand, but she is that way. Or was, I should say. She's been *singing*, Mandy, and love songs of all things! And she's stopped caring about a lot of little things, like polishing the silver and dusting under the clock on the mantle and making me come to the dinner table on time. Then she's been getting letters in the mail every week. And when she gets one, she turns as red as your dress and run away to her room to read it."

"How positively thrilling!" Mandy chirped.

"I don't know what to think of it," Eva admitted. "I'm not used to it, you see. And of course, Grace's gone out of her head over Carter Tankard. It's almost frightening having the two of them this way at the same time."

"Who do you think he is?" Mandy questioned.

"The postman of course!"

"No, no, the fellow who's turned your aunt so!"

"Oh, well," said Eva, "I can't tell. I never get to see the letters she receives. But one time I caught sight of a Portsmouth postmark. I can't think of anyone she knows in Portsmouth except Major Arnold. Even though I've not seen him too often, he's always been very nice to Aunty when he's visited. And he is the sort of fellow I think Aunty would like. You know, he's stern, gentle, respectful. Only I wonder if he's a bit old for her."

"Nonsense!" Mandy argued. "Why, he's the perfect gentleman! I saw him at the Veteran's Tea last week. He'd be quite a catch. Your aunty and he would be the handsomest couple, Eva!"

"Do you really think it's he?" Eva wondered.

"Who else could it be? You said so yourself!"

"I suppose it couldn't be anyone else," Eva said, leaning forward and thoughtfully resting her chin in her hands. "Aunty's not been around many men since my uncle died before I was born."

"I didn't even know she'd been married."

"Well, she never talks about him. I don't know why, but she even took back her maiden name when he died. Oh, Mandy," Eva exclaimed, her face brightening, "wouldn't it be wonderful if she'd found another man to love her again? But do you suppose she has?"

"I think she has, Eva," Mandy grinned. "But why don't you ask her?"

"My goodness, Mandy, I couldn't! Aunty's always been as private as a confession box, she has. I'd never be able to scrape up the cheek to ask a question like that. And anyway, if it's really serious, I'm certain to find out about it eventually."

"Yes, when you discover you've got an uncle!" Mandy giggled.

"An uncle!" Eva repeated musingly. "I've never had an uncle. I wonder if it would almost be like having a—no," she concluded with a sigh, "I don't suppose it would be much like having a father again."

∽⟲

Her name was Priscilla Lucinda Duff. Dainty as a china doll and sweet as an over-sugared gumdrop, she was the envy of half the girls in Southdale School. And she was used to it. As the daughter of Gregory Duff of Duff Housing Agents (and Duff Distributors and Duff Land Offices) and the youngest of three children, she was entirely familiar with the lush life of a pampered child.

Things had never truly been grim for her family. Not only had her father been excused from the draft in accordance with his age, but he also had managed to avoid fighting in the Great War. Thus Priscilla hadn't been bothered by the grief and anxiety of war. In fact, the Second World War actually benefited the Duffs, giving Mr. Duff ample opportunity to increase his wealth while the other men were gone. All in all, Priscilla was used to having things pleasantly her way and getting what she wanted when she so politely asked for it.

She was certainly not used to being rejected.

But rejected she had been, and by Roger Wyatt. Previously, Priscilla had not much cared for the young men in Cot's Haven, for she thought them too common and dull. But when Roger arrived, she secretly became hopelessly infatuated with him, his looks, and his charming ways. She had supposed him an easy conquest, yet he ignored her. Although he was courteous every time she found some discreet excuse for running into him, he never showed any interest in her. He didn't invite her to the cinema, never stopped by her family's lovely home, wouldn't stand and chat with her on the street.

It didn't take long for Priscilla to discover why.

"Why, hallo Harold dear!" Priscilla called one sunny Saturday in late April as she stepped out of Hamill's Dress Shop onto the busy sidewalk.

Harold York was about to hop upon his bicycle by the curb, but when he heard his name, he stopped and looked up.

"What did you call me?" he asked.

"I called you Harold," Priscilla replied, perching bird-like on a bench in front of him. "How are you, dear?"

"Fine," he said, giving her a puzzled look. "And you?"

"Oh, marvelous!" she purred. "Say, have you seen Eva lately by any chance?"

"No, I've been working at Fuller's in the afternoons," he said.

"Fuller's?"

"Fuller's Garage."

"Oh! Yes, what a lovely place. I say, it's too bad you haven't seen Eva. She's such a delightful girl. You know, I've been looking for her this whole week, to invite her to tea at our house; but I always just miss her. She's so very busy now."

"Well, next time I see her I'll tell her you want her," Harold said, swinging a leg over his cycle.

"Oh, that's all right, you needn't," Priscilla replied. "I'm sure Roger Wyatt is much better company than I am."

Harold stopped with his foot on a pedal.

"Roger Wyatt?" he queried. "What's he got to do with Eva?"

"A great deal, I should think. One sees them together rather often, you know."

Harold sat with his forehead wrinkled, staring up the street.

"Well, then," he said at length, shrugging his shoulders, "I suppose you should tell Roger Wyatt that you're looking for Eva. Or you could just telephone. I'm off to Fuller's now."

"Toodle-loo!" the girl sang.

Harold touched his cap and rode away.

"There now," Priscilla said with a fairy's giggle. "That should take care of things nicely."

Major Arnold was a busy man. It was no small task cleaning up after a world war. England kept many of her more experienced men just as occupied rethinking national security and looking for barnacled spies and fifth columnists as they had been planning attacks and overseeing weapons production during wartime. However, though still tasked with serious duties, the major was not out fighting Britain's secret battles against corruption. Nearly a year after V-E Day, Major Arnold discovered he was now on the paperwork end of a long war. And he was becoming increasingly bored filling out forms all day.

One stuffy afternoon in his office, after he had signed his name at least nine hundred times, Arnold sat back in his leather chair, closed his eyes, and took a long, slow sip of his Earl Grey.

"Sir?"

With despair, Arnold looked up at the face of his secretary peeping through his doorway.

"More paperwork, Cummings?" he groaned.

"No sir," the young man replied, stepping in and dropping a stack of envelopes on the desk. "Afternoon post."

"Oh," Arnold grimaced, setting his tea aside and picking up the pile. "Thank you."

Cummings saluted and primly made his exit, leaving the major to peruse the mail. Mechanically, the man shuffled through letter after letter, tossing them into different piles on his desk. But when he reached the end of the stack, he stopped and blinked. One of the envelopes had his name and address written on it in a neat feminine hand that stood in contrast against the dull text of the other business letters. Turning the envelope round, he saw the name Miss Agnes Starbuck written on the back.

"Hmm," he muttered. "This might warrant another look. Hi, Cummings!"

The young man looked in.

"Sir?"

"Get me the case file on Sergeant Ulysses Starbuck."

"Whom?"

"Starbuck!"

His secretary returned several minutes later with a rather thin dossier.

"No, this isn't right," Arnold shook his head, running his eyes over the well-thumbed pages.

"Not right, sir?" Cummings questioned.

"I shouldn't have let you file this with the old cases," Arnold said. "I should have left this right on my desk."

"I understood there was nothing more that could be discovered," the young man observed. "You've had other things to worry about, sir."

"Cummings, there's something you should know," Arnold announced, sweeping up his letter opener and pointing it toward the secretary. "When a man really wants to know something, there is always something more than can be discovered."

"But wasn't the Starbuck incident rather simple, sir?" asked the secretary.

"Relatively."

"Then may I ask why the major wishes to revisit it?"

"Cummings, have you ever walked into a room and felt that things were out of place?" the officer asked. "You couldn't put your finger on it, but you knew something wasn't right. It was as if someone had been there, or an object had been moved or taken."

"Oh yes, sir," the other replied, "I've felt that before. It's very odd."

"Well, every time I've walked into this little room here," he said, motioning to Starbuck's dossier, "I've gotten that feeling. Being a fellow who relies on facts, I've tried to shake it off, but it doesn't go away. Something's not right with this case, Cummings. I don't know what it is, but I know it's there. Someone's moved an object out of place or walked off with it. And I get another feeling, too."

"What's that, sir?"

The major's heavy brow sank down over his narrowing eyes.

"I get the feeling that I've got to find out what it is that's been moved or taken—and that if I don't, someone is going to get hurt."

⌒⟲

His head was as swollen as a zeppelin. Really, he did have some cause for his pride: after years of faulty predictions and groundless insinuations, Mr. Clinton Fraser was actually right. For the past three months, he had discreetly watched that fellow Abernathy (or at least he thought he had done it discreetly), and at last his patience and curiosity had paid off. And so it was with great pride that, armed with his very own eye-witness account, Fraser waltzed into Mulchin's one Saturday afternoon.

"Well, lads, I've done it," he announced, plumping down at the bar.

Since it was early for the usual crowd, only a handful of people were present. None of these individuals bothered to look up from their drinks or food.

"Well?" he said.

As he spoke, Barney came out of the kitchen.

"Oh, it's you, Fraser," he scowled. "Aren't you early?"

"I thought I'd come early," said Fraser, "seein' as how I'll be down at the constabulary the rest o' the night."

"Good for you," Barney shrugged, having heard nothing the old sailor had said.

"D'you know why?" Fraser continued, leaning across the bar and looking down at Barney sorting glasses beneath the counter.

"Why?" Barney asked. "And get off that; I just washed it."

"On account o' the fact that I'll be makin' a statement on Mr. Abernathy," Clint revealed, sitting up smugly.

"Oh, no, not that again!" Barney groaned. "Aren't you ever going to leave that fellow alone?"

"That'd be up to the police," said the sailor, "and maybe even the military."

"Ha! Well, you've finally gone crackers!"

"I mean it, Barney! I've been watchin' that Abernathy for a solid three months, have I, and I finally got a peep into his house this afternoon while he and his missus was away. And you'll never guess what I saw."

"I doubt I will," replied the bartender, "and I don't care, neither. It'd only be more lies and rot."

"Oh, is that how you feel, eh?" Fraser growled indignantly.

"Yes, that's how I feel and how Pat York feels and young Tankard and Benny and Garth at the *Crier* and all the others," Barney broke out, rising hotly. "We're all ruddy sick of it, and I won't deceive you."

"Well, I just won't tell any o' you, then!" Fraser retorted, sliding off his stool.

"Good!"

"You'll regret it!" Clint snarled, shaking his calloused fist in the other man's face. "And so will everyone in Cot's Haven! You'll see! I won't tell a soul what I've seen today. I'd sooner die. And I shouldn't be surprised if you're all comin' with me because o' this, but it'll be on your own heads and that's all!"

"And I do hope that's all," Barney grunted.

With that, Clint Fraser stomped out of that tavern as fast as his sailor's gait would allow.

Barney Mulchin, a good-natured fellow at heart, simply shook his head and laughed the incident off. After all, Fraser hadn't spoken a truth about anything in thirty years. Who could imagine that the meddlesome old salt would have something important to say now?

Chapter 13

Harold was no fool. He might have been dumbfounded by girls sometimes, but he was certainly no fool. He assumed Priscilla Duff had some private, meanspirited purpose for telling him about Eva and Roger Wyatt. Even so, he cared too much for Eva to ignore the other girl's words. And for this reason, he found himself spying on Eva Starbuck.

Really, he did feel badly about it. After all, he was used to being very candid (often to the point of tactless), but this time he felt that waltzing up to his friend and asking her directly about Roger would not produce an honest answer. Still, he hated this little spying job he had undertaken, and it didn't help that he had an uncomfortable feeling that he was doing exactly what Priscilla wanted.

But as time progressed, he hated something else even more. He hated discovering that Priscilla was right. One afternoon he saw Eva and Roger walking together down one of the village streets. Another day he spotted them sitting cozily at a window table in Bordeaux's. The next Saturday they went swimming in the morning and parked their bicycles side by side at the cinema that evening.

What Harold could not understand was why Eva's aunt

was allowing this. He knew what her father, if he were in his right mind, would have to say about this fellow; and he could not imagine that brusque, sensible Agnes Starbuck would feel any differently. But whatever Eva's aunt had to say about this development, Harold York was going to say something of his own before things got too far.

"Well, hallo Eva!" he began, meeting her outside her front door on the first Saturday of May.

"Harold!" she gasped.

"Yes, it's been a while," he smiled.

"Well," she laughed, recovering herself and starting down the steps, "how are things?"

"Oh, all right. And what about you? How's your dad?"

"We're all fine, thanks," Eva replied, trying to step past him.

"Where are you going?"

"Into town, Harold. Why do you ask?" the girl said with a hint of irritation.

"Why shouldn't I?"

Eva looked troubled by his response.

"Well," she returned at length, "I just wondered."

"The truth is, Eva, I heard about this Wyatt fellow," Harold said, deciding now was the time for that bold frontal approach.

Eva's face went pale, and then red, and then pale again.

"How?"

"You've not exactly been meeting in secret."

"What about him, then?" she returned sharply.

"That was my question."

"I don't see why I should tell you," Eva retorted. "I like him, that's all. He's nice."

"He's a bit old," Harold muttered.

"You're only two years younger than he is."

"Well, I'm just your friend," said Harold.

"So is Roger."

"I wonder if he thinks the same of you."

"Now look here, Harold!" Eva erupted like a boiling kettle. "You don't have any right to be asking these questions and making such rude insinuations. I don't know why you've got so nosy and meddlesome. If I happen to walk down the street with a chap, it's certainly no business of yours. So I wish you'd just mind your own shop and stop bothering me about Roger. You're not the only mate I've got in the world, you know, so stop acting like it. It's presumptuous and childish. Now if you don't mind, I've got things to do."

"All right, Eva," said Harold, stepping out of the way.

The girl flounced past him, grabbed her cycle, and speedily made her exit.

Harold stood where he was for a long minute, staring in the direction Eva had gone. Then, despite the freedom of the day and the fair weather, he heaved a sigh and plodded dejectedly home.

"Aren't you running into the village, love?" his mother inquired after she found him slumped back in a sitting room chair.

"No, I don't think so, Mum," he replied.

"Are you sure? It's such a nice day outside."

"It is?" Harold frowned, looking dismally out the window. "Funny, it doesn't seem like such a nice day to me."

~⊙

Everyone present agreed that there couldn't have been a more charming wedding that day. Carter Tankard and his bride may not have been wealthy, but the simple beauty of the ceremony, the creativity and color that graced the church and the little pavilion afterward, and the gracious attention the bride and groom bestowed upon their guests were far more enjoyable than the most lavish gathering without heart.

During the proceedings, Eva couldn't help but notice how her aunt behaved. In the past, Agnes Starbuck had viewed any weddings with general scorn. She had always complained that weddings (and marriage) were extraordinarily overrated and had politely refused any invitation she received to attend one. Eva had expected the same attitude about Grace's marriage, but, to her surprise, her aunt not only accepted the nurse's invitation but also spent most of the event glowing and laughing with the rest of the party. Befuddled, Eva was forced to believe that either her aunt had started drinking or something had dramatically changed her perception of matrimony. Both notions seemed impossible, and yet her aunt's recent behavior pointed firmly to the latter.

"Well," Agnes said as the two strolled homeward from the party that evening, "that was nice, wasn't it?"

"Yes, very," Eva acknowledged.

"Did you see Grace's bouquet?"

"It was quite lovely."

"I'm glad you liked it," her aunt responded. "I did my best in arranging it."

"Aunty! You arranged it?"

"That I did," Agnes grinned.

"I didn't know you liked doing that."

"Well, I do garden, you know. One acquires an eye for that sort of thing. You know, I must admit I didn't expect to go today."

"I didn't think you would, either."

"It's lucky Fran Mulchin didn't feel up to going, or I would have been forced to stay home with your father. But we can't rely on her all the time, you know. Eventually we'll have to find another caretaker."

"But what about Grace?" Eva asked.

"Oh, I think she'll be about a little longer," Agnes answered with a smile, "but I doubt she will stay as long as she planned. I heard her talking to Mrs. Butterfield about taking a position with Dr. McCabe. She mentioned something about better pay and less work. She's got to think more about those things now. We mustn't blame her for that."

"But Daddy needs her!" Eva protested. "He likes Grace. I mean, he likes her as much as he can, I think. He's not afraid of her anymore, and he understands her. What will he do when she leaves?"

"Darling, I don't think he will even notice a difference," Agnes remarked gently. "He's become more withdrawn these past couple months."

"I know," Eva murmured.

"We'll have a new nurse, and you'll see things will be all right," Agnes concluded.

The two walked on in silence for several minutes, smelling the fresh grass and flowers and listening to the wind chattering through new leaves. When they came to their street, Eva was surprised to see Roger Wyatt sitting on their front step.

"Who is that?" asked Agnes, noticing the lad.

Eva was on the verge of saying she didn't know, but she realized that answer certainly wouldn't do.

"He's Roger Wyatt," she replied instead. "You know, he's from across the road."

"Oh, yes, I spoke to Mrs. Wyatt at the wedding party," Agnes recalled. "But I wonder what he's doing at our house."

By this time, they were so close that Roger stood up and waved.

"Hallo, Eva!" he called, walking their way.

Eva waved hesitantly back.

"I say, wasn't the wedding a smash? The cake was first-rate," he commented cheerily as he approached. "Hallo, I'm Roger Wyatt," he added, extending a friendly hand to Eva's aunt.

"Oh, Roger, this is my aunt Agnes," Eva said hurriedly. "Aunty, this is Roger Wyatt."

"Ready to go, Eva?" the boy questioned after the usual amenities had been exchanged. "We'll just arrive before it gets crowded."

"In a minute," Eva replied, nervously noting the expression on her aunt's face.

"I'll wait here," Roger offered.

Eva hastened into the house, followed closely by Agnes.

"How well do you know that young man?" Agnes said, stopping her in the hall.

"Oh, we met a while ago. Harold introduced us," Eva explained casually. "The three of us are going into the village together."

"Harold, eh?"

"Yes."

Agnes looked contemplative for a moment, but then she waved off her concern.

"Well, all right then, if it's Harold and all," she decided. "Have a nice time!"

"Thanks!" the girl replied as she dashed to her room to change.

Eva didn't look her aunt in the eye when she thanked her. She could not: Eva Starbuck hadn't lied to anyone years.

∽๑

Grace's announcement of departure came sooner than expected. She acted rather ashamed about it when she approached Agnes a couple weeks after her marriage, but Agnes was entirely understanding and even supportive of the young nurse's choice to take a position as Dr. McCabe's new assistant.

Eva was not. Although Grace promised to stay on until a replacement was found, Eva still felt that the older girl had abandoned her father. However, whether Eva liked it or not, Agnes engaged a new caretaker only a week after Grace gave notice.

This new caretaker took some getting used to. Eva was accustomed to coming home to Grace's cheery voice and smiling face. Instead, each day after school Eva walked through the front door to be greeted by a stern face, a sharp Scot's tongue, and two piercing gray eyes that made the girl feel unnervingly guilty.

Mrs. Sally Abernathy was the lady's name. A retired nurse of thirty years, she was the picture of efficiency and frugality in every respect. She also possessed an extremely sour disposition which she daily flung at everyone but Agnes and her patient. If it weren't for the fact that the lady behaved both gently and kindly to Ulysses, Eva would have found Mrs. Abernathy intolerable.

Luckily, Eva was not at home too often to speak to the caregiver. It was one of those lovely warm Junes only England can produce; and the vivid green hues and wild sea air were far too invigorating to keep a child indoors. But there were other reasons for staying outside. For one thing, there was only a month left of the school term, and the incredible itch to finish made it difficult to study. And, of course, there was Roger.

Once upon a time, Eva hardly cared that boys existed. To her, boys were bothersome, rough, and rude. Now, Harold was a bit different, for he was not *quite* so bothersome and rough and rude as the others. But he had only been a friend to have adventures with when girls like Mandy wanted to talk about tedious things like make-up and cheap, sappy novels. Harold was just Harold and didn't count as a boy.

Her father had been her true first love, the only man she thought worth admiring or holding hands with or kissing. When Ulysses was lost, there was a terrible void left behind in Eva. His return didn't fill it. And then one day there stepped into that void the kind, clever, handsome Roger Wyatt. So naturally did he step in that Eva felt he was always meant to be there.

Mandy Butterfield thought the whole thing was positively thrilling. She swore by the novel *Rosy Wilson's First Love* (and its sequel *Rosy Wilson's Second First Love*) that Eva and Roger were doubtless meant for one another and would probably be dramatically separated for five years and then marry after discovering one another again in Vienna.

Mandy may have known about Roger, but Eva's aunt could not have resided more in the dark. Through the beginning of June, Agnes was in a state of nervous agitation, both at home and at work. By the middle of the month, she was almost frantic. After being waved off with a flurried "nothing's the matter" a few times, Eva gave up questioning Agnes and decided that her aunt's behavior had something to do with this mysterious man writing her letters.

One late afternoon, after an exceptionally agitated day, Agnes came home and immediately announced that she was going out again that evening and would not be back until the next morning.

"Where are you going?" Eva queried.

"Portsmouth, dear," was her aunt's reply. "I'll probably be back before you wake up tomorrow. Mrs. Abernathy will stay the night. I'm sorry I can't take you with me."

"Oh, don't worry, I've got things to do," said Eva.

"Well, that's good," Agnes smiled, appearing relieved.

"By the way, I know you're going to be off and all," Eva went on, "but do you mind if I say goodbye after dinner and leave straight afterward? Harold asked me to go to the cinema with him to see *Arabian Knights*. I've finished all my studies and chores for the day. Is that all right?"

"Certainly," her aunt replied.

When dinnertime came, Eva ate as fast as her aunt and Mrs. Abernathy would allow, kissed Agnes farewell, and then skipped out the door. She had not been gone ten minutes before the bell rang.

"Why, Harold!" Agnes greeted the boy standing on the mat.

"Hallo, Miss Starbuck, is Eva home?" said Harold.

"I'm afraid she's probably asking your mother the same thing," Agnes chuckled.

"Asking for me?" Harold wondered, hope glinting in his eyes.

"Yes, she went to meet you not fifteen minutes ago. She'll probably ride to the cinema when she doesn't find you. I should go there to look for her if I were you."

"Cinema?"

"Yes, if you two are going to see *Arabian Knights*, you'd better get there soon. Eva mentioned it starts at half past seven. And do be sure Eva's home before nine."

"Miss Starbuck, I—"

"I'm sorry, I don't need to ask you that, do I?" Agnes smiled kindly. "You and your family have always been very good to Eva, Harold. Ulysses and I never had to worry about her if one of the Yorks was with her. Of course, she'll be back before nine."

"Yes, mum," Harold acknowledged.

Soon the boy was speeding down the road on his cycle.

"Yes, sir," he muttered firmly to himself as the houses flashed by. "By Jove, Harold York will bring her back before nine."

⌒◯

Harold did not get upset very often, but by the time he swerved puffing up to the Telescope that Friday evening, he could honestly say he was angry. Fiercely, he shoved his cycle into the nearest rack and glanced up and down the rows of bicycles lined up beside the theater. It only took a moment to spot Eva's: just as Harold suspected, it was snuggled up next to Roger Wyatt's machine.

The boy's anger turned nearly to fury. He ran to the ticket booth, expecting to see a crowd full of children patiently waiting entry to *Arabian Knights*. Instead, he found a line of couples who seemed too old to be interested in such a film.

Harold looked up at the marquee:

LOVE IN ATHENS: 7:30

"By Jove," the boy growled.

Rapidly, he scanned the faces in the crowd, hoping to spot Eva and Roger. But the two were not among them. They must have already gone into the building.

Harold was desperate. Just entering the cinema would take an eternity if he stood in line, but if he tried waltzing in without a ticket he would surely be turned out on his ear. There was only one alternative.

A couple years ago, one of his schoolmates had shown him a side door in the alley that led to the theater's silver screen. The other boy had often sneaked in that way to watch the films without a ticket. Now, as sordid as it was, Harold was prepared to get into the Telescope that way.

Love in Athens was not a lovely film. Eva's mother would likely have done a few turns in her grave if she knew what her daughter was watching that evening. In fact, at any other time Eva herself would have avoided it as garbage. But Roger had suggested it, and somehow everything looked wonderful when Roger suggested it.

Early in the film, Roger got up to buy his girl some candy,

leaving an empty seat beside Eva. Eva had not been staring blankly at the screen for more than five seconds before she felt a breath of warm air tickle her ear.

"Eva!"

Eva flinched and looked round.

"Harold, what on earth?" she said with a squeak.

"What the devil are you doing here?" the boy growled. "You told your aunt that you were here with me! How could you, Eva? How could you lie like that?"

"I—"

"And you're watching *this* rot!" Harold seethed, poking a passionately quivering finger at the screen. "I never dreamed you'd do something like this! Using me, taking advantage of your aunt, of your own father!"

"Oh, please stop!" Eva whimpered, grasping his arm.

In the dim light, Harold caught the reflection of a tear trickling down the girl's face.

"Please, I'm sorry!" she said. "I really am, Harold! I won't do it again. Just don't tell Aunty about this. I want to do it on my own. I need to, Harold."

"You'll tell her, then?" he asked. "Everything?"

"Yes, yes!"

"Promise?"

"I do!"

Harold leaned over and looked her in the face.

"Eva, I mean it. Do you promise?"

Rubbing a tear from her cheek, the girl nodded vigorously.

Harold sat silent for a moment; then he shook his head.

"All right, then," he spoke at last. "But you've got to get out of here now."

"But what shall I tell Roger?"

"I've got a thing or two I'd like to tell him," Harold scowled.

"But why don't you say this film is rubbish and you don't want to watch it?"

"But Harold!"

"Eva!"

"Oh fine, I will," the girl gave in.

"Good, that's settled," the boy concluded. "Now shall we get an ice cream?"

"We?"

"Yes, we," Harold returned. "I promised your aunt I'd have you home before nine, and that's what I intend to do."

❧

Major Arnold was enveloped in a cloud of cigarette smoke. For hours, he had sat hunched over his desk, flipping through papers, writing notes, reading the same pages repeatedly. The night was old, but he was not about to leave the office.

"Cummings!" he shouted.

There was no answer. Arnold looked at his watch: it was one o' clock. His secretary must have left long ago. Rising in agitation, the major stuffed the stub of a cigarette into an ashtray heaped with debris and smoldering like Mount Saint Helens. With a groan, he straightened his stiff back and wandered over to the coffee pot.

It was empty.

"Blast," he growled, rubbing his disheveled hair.

Just then there was a thump on the frosted glass of his door.

"Come in!" he yelled.

"Eh, telegram, sir?" said a boy, stepping in.

"Yes!" the man cried, snatching the item from the lad and shoving some change into his hands. "Out, out!" he ordered when the messenger stopped to count the money.

As the lad scuttled off, the major tore the envelope open

and fervidly scanned the enclosed contents. His eyes widened an instant before narrowing intensely.

"Utter fools," he rumbled. "How could we have been so blind?"

Abruptly, he threw down the paper, put on his coat and cap, and barreled out of the office, slamming the door behind him.

He had forgotten to turn out the lamp. In its warm light, anyone might have seen the crumpled telegram still lying on the desk and emblazoned with the following words:

MARVIN SHORT DEAD = THIS MAN IMPOSTER.

Chapter 14

When Eva awoke Saturday morning, she expected to find her aunt back at home. Instead, she found a laconic note on the kitchen table:

> E:
> At grocers. Father had breakfast already. Make your own. Aunt called: detained, will be back in a week. I will be staying in her absence.
>
> —S.A.

"Aunty gone a week!" Eva exclaimed. "But why?"

Sighing, she poked her head into the icebox and frowned. Ever since Mrs. Abernathy started taking charge of the groceries, hardly anything looked appetizing. The only things that woman was capable of purchasing were flour, oats, and potatoes. There was not a hearty bit of English sausage or a friendly side of English bacon in sight.

"Well, there's always lunch," she reasoned, and wandered out of the kitchen and into the sitting room.

Staring out the bow window at the sunlight dancing on Roger Wyatt's roof, Eva gradually got the feeling that she was not alone in the house. In fact, she was not alone in that very room. Her muscles started to tighten, and she felt the hair stiffen on the back of her neck.

A floorboard on the other side of the room creaked. Eva jerked around—and there he was. Without a glance in her direction, he shambled to the sofa and dropped down upon it.

For a moment, she had not recognized her father. Thanks to Mrs. Abernathy, he was perhaps more neatly dressed and well-groomed than before, but that wasn't what made him seem different. And then Eva realized that, although she had seen her father every day for weeks, during that time she had not really thought about him. It was as if she had forgotten he existed. And now, there he was, drooping over in that same old spot, still existing, still alive in some sense, and still not at home.

Slowly, Eva stood, walked to her father, and touched his shoulder. She expected him to lurch back as he had before, but he did nothing.

"Daddy," she started, but the doorbell interrupted her.

Before she could see who it was, the door opened and in strolled Roger.

"Good morning, Eva!" he said in his usual cheery manner.

"Roger Wyatt, you should have knocked!" Eva remonstrated, tying the cord of her robe and frantically finger-combing her wild curls.

"I did," he smiled. "Or I rang, really."

"Yes, but you should have let me open the door!"

"I'm sorry," he shrugged. "I came to see if you'd like to come over for breakfast. It's just Mum and me, since Dad's gone in to work early. Since you left so quickly last night, I thought we'd make up for lost time. And I say, is this your father?" Roger asked, gesturing toward Ulysses.

"Yes," Eva said hesitantly.

"Well, I've been looking forward to meeting you, sir," Roger proclaimed, gallantly taking one of Ulysses' limp hands and giving it a firm squeeze. "Roger Wyatt, from across the road."

"He can't hear you, Roger."

"Oh, I don't know about that," the boy replied. "Don't you think we should behave like he can?"

Eva stared at Roger for at least ten seconds.

"I thought you'd make fun of him," she stammered.

"Eva!" Roger chided. "What nonsense! I should never do such a thing. Why, didn't you tell me what a dreadful time he had of it? You know I had family in the war, too. I could never poke fun at anyone like that."

"Roger, you're wonderful!" Eva beamed.

"Not at all. Now, are you coming to breakfast?"

"Oh, I want to, but I can't," the girl sighed. "The nurse is out shopping and Aunty's in Portsmouth for the week."

"I don't understand."

"Well, someone should be home with Daddy."

"Won't he be fine?"

Eva looked at her father.

"Well, he never does much anyway," she admitted.

"Then he'll be fine," Roger concluded. "Won't you, sir? Why, you'll not be gone twenty minutes, Eva, and you'll only be across the street. Can't you spare her that long, Mr. Starbuck?" the boy asked, smiling at her father.

"Well, I suppose it's all right, then," the girl decided. "Just let me go and change."

After Eva had gone to her room, Roger bent down and looked more closely at Ulysses.

"So," he said at length, "you're the chap who's come back from the dead. You're rather fortunate, you know. Most people who die don't come back."

He said the words with a congenial grin on his face; but there was something uncanny about his voice tone, something unsettling about the look in his eyes.

"I'm ready!" Eva sang, bouncing back into the room.

"Lovely as ever," the boy remarked, straightening hastily. "Shall we go?"

"Yes, in a moment."

Hesitantly, Eva touched her father's shoulder. He still did not respond.

"I'll be right back, Daddy," she said. "You'll be all right."

"Of course he shall," Roger asserted.

In a minute, the boy had whisked Eva away.

The house was still for a quarter of an hour before the telephone rang. It rang—and rang—and rang. But no one answered it. Ulysses sat where Eva had left him, staring down at the floor, completely unmoved by the desperate trills that echoed through the house. Whoever was calling would have to wait, for, by all accounts, everyone in that house was away.

"I missed her again?" Eva whined the next day when she found out her aunt had called in her absence.

"Aye, and that's no one's fault but yers!" Mrs. Abernathy returned sharply. "Runnin' about all day and such. Don't ye complain t' me! If ye want t' talk t' her, stay at home!"

"You don't want me around," Eva retorted.

"No more than ye want t' be around."

"Well, what did she say was keeping her?" Eva asked to change to subject.

"She dinna say, and I dinna ask her," Mrs. Abernathy replied crustily. "It wasn't my business."

"What did she say, then?"

"What's not yer business."

Rankled, Eva left the house as soon as possible. How that woman could be so frosty with her and so benevolent to her father was incredible.

Ah, yes, her father. Thinking of him sent a twinge of guilt through Eva, not only because she had inadvertently ignored him but also because she had left him alone the day before. But after all, it was not as if he noticed any of that. It would be different if her company made an impact upon him, but it did not. Whatever effect Morton Euston had generated last year was certainly transient. It was a coincidence. And all the patient care Agnes, Grace, and Eva had given Ulysses in the past several months had been utterly fruitless.

The fact was Eva's father had died nearly a year ago. What she lived with every day was only his ghost. And no one needed to feel guilty for ignoring a ghost.

Eva was truly bored that day. She hated the thought of going back home to Mrs. Abernathy, but she was struggling to find something to do elsewhere. She first stopped by the grocers to see Roger, but he was, strangely enough, in a bad temper and told her he would be working all day. A call to Mandy only produced Mrs. Butterfield, who said her daughter had gone to Brighton with the Duffs for the weekend and wouldn't be back until Monday. So, Eva went down to the beach.

It was a gorgeous day for a walk. The sky was clear of the usual blanket of clouds, the breeze from the sea was strikingly fresh, and the gulls were dancing and diving and mewing at one another along the shore. But Eva was not in the mood to notice any of this. She was mad at Mrs. Abernathy. She was puzzled by her aunt's secretive absence. She was offended that Mandy did not even tell her she was leaving. And she was both confused and hurt by Roger's curt behavior.

Furthermore, she did not like being alone. But who else was there to be with?

"Afternoon, Eva!"

Eva looked up and saw Harold York.

"Good afternoon," she said, trying a half-hearted smile.

"What are you doing by the pier today?" he asked, hopping out of a small boat tied to the dock.

"Oh," Eva said, looking round, "I suppose I am at the pier, aren't I? I was just walking along."

"By yourself?" Harold noted.

"Yes."

"Where's Roger, then?"

"At the grocer's," Eva replied.

"I suppose you're going off with him this evening," Harold said, wiping his fishy hands on a handkerchief.

"Yes, probably," Eva lied.

"Then your aunt must think he's all right."

"Yes, she thinks he's very nice," said Eva. "Have you been fishing today?"

"Even after you told her about the cinema?" Harold questioned.

"Sure! I mean, actually I haven't told her yet."

"Eva!"

"I couldn't help it, Harold!" Eva protested. "She left for Portsmouth before I got home that night, and she hasn't come back yet. I'll tell her when she gets back, I promise!"

"Does she even know you're running about with that scoundrel?" the boy pressed.

"Of course she does! How could she not? And Roger is not

a scoundrel, so I would appreciate it if you didn't talk about him that way!"

"Well, I'm of a mind he is," Harold returned imperturbably. "There's something wrong with him. I don't think your dad would like him at all."

"Don't tell me what you think my father would or wouldn't like," Eva fumed. "Daddy would have liked Roger. Roger is a perfect gentleman, and Daddy would have seen that. He wouldn't be always hounding me and poking at me about Roger like you do, Harold! You don't even know him, and yet you stand here all high and mighty and call him a scoundrel! You're jealous, that's what you are, because I'm in love with Roger."

"In love!" Harold echoed. "Don't you think it's a bit early to think that?"

"Certainly not! I'm entirely in love with Roger. Maybe you don't know anything about falling in love."

"I daresay you don't either!" Harold blurted, losing his self-control. "You couldn't!"

"I could and I do!" Eva shot back.

"You just couldn't fall in love with him, Eva!" Harold insisted. "You're just a little girl, and you don't know what you're talking about. You just think you've fallen in love with him, and sooner or later you'll realize you were wrong."

"What kind of a fool do you think I am?" Eva exploded. "I know what I feel, and just because you can't wrap your mind around it doesn't mean it's not true! I'm ruddy in love with Roger, and that's an end of it!"

Harold took a step back and sat down weakly onto one of the dock steps. Still livid, Eva stomped away in rage.

"She couldn't," Harold whispered to himself. "No, no, no, she just couldn't! She only thinks she has! She'll get over it, she will. Eva's a good girl. She'll soon see what's wrong, and then she'll be all right again. Please God," he said miserably, "she's just got to be all right again."

∽◯

Gregory Duff flumped into his favorite easy chair in the sitting room and put up his slippered feet.

"A drink, darling?" his wife Janelle offered, handing him his paper.

"Quite," he replied, running his eyes over the front page of the *Manchester Guardian.*

"How was your day?" she asked, mixing his beverage.

"As well as can be expected with the recent surplus of useless new employees," Duff grunted. "Cochrane said we should give positions to some of those soldiers back from the war, for good public relations and all; but so far I've found them all intolerably stupid. Never a bigger lot of—Priscilla, where have you been?"

Mr. Duff broke off his rant when he noticed his daughter sweeping past the sitting room doorway.

"What, Father?" the girl inquired, poking her head into the room.

"Where have you been all afternoon?" the man asked. "Miss Hattering tells me you missed your piano lesson. Of course, I had to pay for it anyway."

"Sorry, Father, but I was out with a friend and couldn't make it back in time."

"Which friend, I wonder?"

"Ah, probably that Mandy Butterfield," said Mrs. Duff with a knowing smile. "She's a sweet child. I did enjoy having her along to Brighton over the weekend."

"Even if she *is* common," Priscilla put in hastily, seeing the disgusted glower forming on her father's face.

"Well, there are worse sorts in this village," Mr. Duff observed.

"At least the Butterfield child isn't subnormal. Better to be common than that. No daughter of mine shall be found in the company of someone like that, and so I say it. A fine lot of burdens to decent folk those people are. Don't you think so, Janelle?"

"One does wonder," his wife admitted.

"Why, think of all those half-balmy soldiers sent home from the war!" Duff exclaimed. "Like the ones Cochrane brought in. Utterly useless! Or that Ulysses Starbuck that worked at the factory. Never the brightest pebble, I always said, but now that the Germans have minced his brains, he's positively pathetic.

"Only yesterday I was passing by the park, and I saw him with that old nurse Abernathy. Sitting on one of the benches, he was, his head cocked over to one side like his neck was broken, gazing about with the most senile, witless expression. Why, drooling he was, and on one of the benches we useful citizens paid for!

"I tell you, after a war they send back all these weak-minded burdens on society, and all they do is trouble and burden their families and villages. They've no use at all. Sometimes I can't help but wonder if the Nazis didn't have a good notion when—"

"Ahem!" said Mrs. Duff, looking hard at her husband and motioning her head toward their daughter.

"Oh, yes," Priscilla's father stuttered, glancing at her. "Well, anyway, I don't know why Agnes Starbuck doesn't send him away, Janelle. She has some sense, I think. Do the whole village good, removing an eyesore that could be dangerous."

"Dangerous!" Priscilla said.

"Ah, yes, quite. You keep clear of him, Priscilla. One never knows what a fellow like that is capable of. One just never does."

᧒

It was cold. And it smelled like mold and stale sweat. He was hungry, too; it had been at least two days since he had eaten. Or maybe it was three. He had lost count, really. And anyway, he was mostly thirsty. Looking down at his long, shaky fingers, he thought to himself that a few shots of whisky would be fine about now. He was just thinking of asking the constable if a couple quid would send him off for some when there was a grinding noise, and the metal door at the end of the room swung open.

In walked a tall, mustached gentleman. After looking Short over with a cool eye, the man sat down at the other end of the table and dropped a couple files onto it.

"Well," he said, folding his arms across his bemedaled breast, "we meet again, Private Short. You look well, sir."

The young man, white as new linen and thin as a fence pole, brought his trembling hands into his lap.

"Major Arnold," he muttered. "What are you doing here?"

"Looking for you," said the officer. "The constable told me you've been charged with drunken and disorderly conduct. That is unfortunate."

"I lose track of myself sometimes," Short replied. "No crime drinking a little, though. I wish they'd let me go now."

"They might. I thought of posting your bail," Arnold continued, "provided you do me a favor."

"Anything!" Short exclaimed. "I've got to get out of here. It's terrible conditions, Major, and I'm dying for a drink. Oh, I'd be so grateful, sir!"

"If it means that much to you, I suppose you won't mind telling me the truth."

As he spoke, Arnold produced a fire-singed, yellowed piece of paper from one of the files and slid it across the table.

"Do you see what's circled in the middle?"

Short looked down at the sheet and mouthed a yes.

"Can you read German?"

"No, sir. I—I don't understand. The truth about what?"

"You, Mr. Short," Arnold replied. "Of course, I can't guarantee telling me the truth will be in your favor. But I can assure you of something else: if you lie to me, I will personally use every means at my disposal to drag you into prison and drop the key to your cell into the Atlantic. Now, this paper reads, '10 March 1945: Selkirk called. Selkirk executed.' Are you ready to talk?"

"I—I could do with a whisky first," the young man mumbled.

"Well, it's only too bad about your bail, then."

"All right," Short moaned, "I'll talk."

"Good," said the major, leaning forward and folding his hands in front of him. "Now then, Mr. Marvin Selkirk, this time let's have the truth."

Chapter 15

"I'm goin' out t'night," announced Mrs. Abernathy. "I'll be back by t'morrow mornin'."

"Tomorrow morning!" Eva responded, looked up from her boiled egg and toast. "But Aunty said you were to spend days and nights here until she got back."

"I'm takin' a night t' myself, lass," the lady replied with her usual glower. "I have a husband and a home, neither of which I've seen these past three days."

"But what about Daddy?"

"He'll have his dinner before I go, and I'll be back in time fer breakfast," was the terse reply.

"But he's not supposed to be alone."

"He won't be alone if yer home, no' will he?" said the nurse.

Eva could not argue that, but she made a mental note to tell Agnes about this the next time her aunt called. That loathsome woman didn't deserve to be paid for a night she spent at home.

Later that evening, Eva came back from studying in the park and found Mrs. Abernathy tapping her foot on the steps.

"Well, it's about time!" the lady growled, snatching up her carpetbag.

Muttering some sharp Scottish insults, the woman stomped past the girl and marched off down the street.

It felt odd and empty going into that house, almost as it had felt last Christmas. A cold and meager dinner was awaiting Eva on the kitchen sideboard. Judging by the mound of dirty dishes the nurse had left in her haste, it was apparent that the girl was eating alone tonight.

She was halfway through her meal and staring at fading twilight through the kitchen windows when a face shot up against the windowpane. The first thing Eva did was squeal. The second was to hurry to the kitchen door and throw it open.

"If you do that again, Roger, you'll kill me!" she reprimanded the boy as he came in.

"Not likely," he said. "And say, I'm dreadful sorry about how I acted yesterday. I was miffed over one or two bad customers, that's all."

"Well, I forgive you," Eva smiled.

"What about calling it pax by listening to the village band tonight?" the boy asked. "We can get there early and sit in front."

"Mrs. Abernathy's gone home for the night," Eva frowned.

"The night?"

"Yes, and she wasn't supposed to, either," Eva grumbled. "I've got a mind to tell Aunty before she gets back. That'll fix her."

"Well," said Roger, "who's staying here with you?"

"Daddy."

"But who's staying with him?"

"I am."

"I say, is that safe?" the boy asked with concern.

"Oh, very," Eva reassured him. "Daddy's just going to sit about for a while and then go to bed. I think I can handle that."

"He's not dangerous then?" Roger questioned.

"Not at all."

"Well!" Roger chuckled, flashing his pearly teeth. "Shall we go?"

"You know I can't, Roger!"

"Nonsense! Just an hour."

"No, this time I can't," Eva said firmly. "That's much too long."

For an instant, Roger's countenance grew angry, but then it softened into that same winsome smile once again.

"Well, that's all right, then," he said, shrugging his shoulders carelessly. "Maybe if we sit out on the steps together, we'll hear a bit of the music, eh?"

"That sounds nice," Eva agreed happily. "Just let me put these things away, and I'll be with you directly."

While Eva was taking care of a few dishes, Roger wandered out of the kitchen into the sitting room. There was Ulysses, sitting in that same old spot in the same old position. The boy wondered if he ever did anything else.

"Well," he said, strolling over to him, "good evening, Mr. Starbuck. How nice to see you again!"

Of course, the man did not acknowledge the greeting. But Roger didn't care. As he stood looking at the man, his sunny face gradually hardened into cold eyes and a tight jaw. Bending down, he leaned forward so close to Ulysses' ear that their faces nearly touched.

"I just want you to know," he hissed, his voice tense as the moment before a thunderstorm, "I'm wise to your little secret, Starbuck. I know what you did in that prison camp. I know you're not a hero, or a victim. You and I both know what you are. I'm here to even the score. Whatever it takes, I'll make sure you're punished for what you did to my brother."

"Oh, there you are!" Eva said, coming unexpectedly from the kitchen. "Talking to Daddy again? Dear Roger, even after I told you he doesn't hear you."

"You never know," said the boy again, glancing at Ulysses and offering Eva his hand. "Now let's go and sit on the steps."

As the two young people were leaving the room, neither bothered to look back at Eva's father. After all, there was nothing to see except that same languid face and shrunken form. Little did they know that those dulled eyes were now narrowed and alert as they stared after the children, and that the man's vacant countenance was instead exchanged for a face contorted with the most alarming hatred.

⌒᠍᠍᠍᠍᠍᠍᠍◦

"To be honest, sir, I'm not satisfied," said Major Arnold.

The man he addressed, a heavily built general with even heavier eyebrows, looked up from the papers before him.

"Not satisfied?" he asked. "Why not? From what I've read of the case, it's rather self-explanatory. Not that cowardice and desertion of a comrade are anything to be sneezed at, you understand, but it appears like nothing more. This—Selkirk, was it?—steals Private Short's tags after Short dies in the camp and plans to hide from execution under the name of the dead man. Rather a feeble blind, I might say, but it worked. Then he becomes ashamed of what he's done and covers his actions by masquerading as Marvin Short and praying that no one will discover the truth until it doesn't matter any longer."

"It's more than that, General," said the major.

"Ah, Arnold, I haven't forgotten the lie about his sergeant being dead," the general nodded. "Such cowardice is sickening, sir. It's unworthy of the British Army, of an Englishman! To leave a man to die alone and unnamed because he slows you down and eats your food is a crime we shan't tolerate!

"Even so, the war is over. We have more important things to worry about in the Army. So do you, Major. If I were you, I

144

shouldn't waste so much time tying up loose ends and sweeping up casualties. You can't make an omelet, you know, without breaking some eggs. Such things happen in war."

"These loose ends and eggs you refer to are men," returned the major.

"Tens of thousands of men are still lost," the general rumbled. "Are you going to bring them all home, tend their injuries, bury the dead, and give each man the justice he deserves? Are you going to Das Grab and dig up every grave and carve every headstone? Of course you shan't!"

"No, sir," replied Arnold through his teeth.

"I know you were a prisoner during the Great War, Major," said the general, his demeanor softening a touch. "And I know you lost your nephew to Das Grab."

"Begging the general's pardon," Arnold corrected, clenching his fists behind him, "but we don't know Lieutenant Ryder is dead any more than we know that the commandant of Das Grab is dead. Most of the camp's records were burned."

The general looked at Arnold and heaved a sigh.

"What do you want then, Major?" he asked at last.

"I'm convinced Selkirk is withholding something," Arnold responded, "and I believe what he's withholding is important. I ask your permission to continue this line of inquiry to the end."

"You really won't give up on this, eh?"

"Not until I get the whole truth."

"Well, if you insist, go ahead. I trust your judgment, though I doubt you'll find out much more than the fact that Selkirk stole rations from his comrades and cheated at cards. But let me remind you, Major, that it's the missing commandant of Das Grab that the British Army really wants. A man who erects his own private stalag in the mountains of Germany and spirits away Allied soldiers from other camps to kill them in the most diabolical ways is far more dangerous than a small worm like Selkirk."

"I want them both held accountable, sir," said the other officer.

"Ha!" laughed the general. "Thorough Major Arnold, I doubt you will get them both. But who knows? We might all be surprised before the day is over."

∽♉∾

"Aunty, what on earth are you doing?" Eva asked, eagerly pressing the telephone receiver closer to her ear. "It's been five days, and I haven't talked to you once!"

"I'm sorry, darling!" her aunt's voice crackled back. "I called several times, but you were always out. I'll be home Saturday morning, love, I promise!"

"But what are you doing?"

"I'll explain it when I come home, sweetheart. I'm in Torquay right now, at the Yellow Piers, if you need to telephone me."

"Torquay!" Eva returned. "I thought you were in Portsmouth, Aunty!"

"I was at first. I'll explain later. I've got to be off now, dear. Tell me quickly how you and your father are!"

"We're fine, but Mrs. Abernathy is terrible."

"Oh, I know, darling, she's rather beastly to you," Agnes admitted. "I'll call tomorrow and talk to her about it. Will you be all right until then?"

"Well," Eva hesitated, "yes, I suppose I will."

"Remember to call the Yorks if you need them."

"Oh. Yes."

"Miss you awfully, dear. I'll see you Saturday morning! Goodbye now!"

"Bye," Eva murmured, returning the receiver to its cradle.

She just could not understand any of this. Her aunt was so different, going places without telling anyone why or where, talking with that flurried, giddy voice. And Torquay of all places! She could hardly imagine a woman like Agnes Starbuck staying at Torquay for any reason.

"Three days," she told herself. "Three days and it will finally make sense."

In the meantime, Eva had plenty of other things to do.

∽⟡

"The game's up, Selkirk," Arnold disclosed as he shoved his way into the young man's dingy flat. "It's all out."

Selkirk, trembling and sweating for liquor, staggered back and sat upon his bed.

"It's right here," the major went on, patting a folder he had brought with him. "Every bit of it, the story of your life in Das Grab."

At first Selkirk stared blankly at the man, but then he understood what was said.

"All of it?" he asked, his pupils dilating.

"Everything."

"You're joking."

"I am not," the officer replied, closing the door and leaning against it. "I have everything but what was going on in your twisted skull during that time. You have only one chance to save yourself, Selkirk."

"What is it?" the young man cried, rifling through his bedclothes for a bottle.

"Tell me why you did it. Explain all of it."

"What about a lawyer?"

"What lawyer?"

"Oh, no!"

"Go ahead," Arnold pressed impatiently. "The truth is the only thing left that can save you."

Selkirk sat on his lumpy mattress, rocking back and forth and moaning over an empty whisky bottle for a least a minute. The major was just about to turn and feign an exit when the young man burst into tears and groaned out, "I'll tell you!"

"Well?" demanded the officer.

"I didn't want to die!" Selkirk spluttered, quaking all over. "We all knew my name was coming up. The commandant had chosen the S's that month, and they'd already killed Sanders and Selden, they had! But I had the escape all planned. I just needed more time and I'd be out! I had to have more time! You see that, don't you?"

Arnold stared impassively at the other man.

"You weren't there," Selkirk went on wretchedly. "You didn't see how the others died. They killed them right in front of us, and they laughed the whole time! It was awful enough seeing men dying every day and night from starvation and cold and thirst and failed escapes and that horrid Standing Line; but when he started ordering men murdered this new way, I swear to heaven it was more than mortals were meant to take! I couldn't go like that, I just couldn't!"

Selkirk paused, panting and wiping the sweat from his face.

"Go on," Arnold directed.

"He said there was only one way out," the youth continued, drawing his sleeve across his nose. "He said I'd have to swap with someone. He said it wasn't murder because the chap he'd pick would be as good as dead anyway. I was so scared, sir, that I listened to him. I didn't think about it! I couldn't! I just did what he said.

"So, one night I crawled over to Marvin Short's bunk. I hadn't a thing in the world against him. But he was dying so fast we didn't expect him to live to see the morning. I took his tags and gave him mine while he was asleep. I wouldn't have done it, but he said the chap wouldn't live to hear my name called up. And it was called, the very next day! Oh, but I couldn't have known! I was digging graves on the north side of the camp (they'd ordered Short for that work) when they brought my name up. And he was still alive!

"I didn't see it, but *he* did, and he said it was the worst. 'You're a lucky one,' he told me. 'If it weren't for me, you'd have died that way.' I can't tell you how horrible I felt about it. But I had to get out of there. And so, a couple days later when they would have called for Marvin Short, by God's mercy I was already gone."

The young man leaned forward and buried his face in his hands.

It was a long five minutes before Major Arnold spoke. When he did, his voice was flat and expressionless.

"Who."

Selkirk looked up and swallowed a sob.

"Who?" the youth echoed.

"Who was it?"

"What do you mean?"

"The man who told you to switch tags," Arnold said, "the man who so coldly exchanged another man's life for yours—who was he?"

The youth licked his crusted lips and hesitated.

"Selkirk, you killed a man," said the major.

"It," the youth murmured, "it was the sergeant."

"Sergeant Starbuck?"

"Yes."

"All right, then."

Major Arnold did not say another word. Stiffly, he opened the folder he had brought in and dumped several sheets of blank paper onto the floor. Then he opened the door and left the flat.

Chapter 16

It was a perfectly normal Friday evening. Eva had spent most of that afternoon putting her bedroom and the bathroom back in place. Unintentionally, she had let her house chores slide rather badly in her aunt's absence, and it took sweat and determination to reorder things. Now, after dinner and homework, it was time to curl up with a good book and relax before bed.

Contentedly, Eva snuggled into her favorite chair next to the open window in her room, flipped on the table lamp, and eagerly turned to Chapter 14 in Mandy's well-thumbed copy of *Rosy Wilson's First Love*:

> *Rosy's heart was so full that a smile could have burst it.*
> *Her mind was brimming over with the vivid memories*
> *of Alistair's marriage proposal, and–*

"I'm off."

Eva looked up.

"You're not leaving again!" she exclaimed.

"I am," said the nurse.

"You know I could tell Aunty all about this," Eva challenged as politely as she could.

"And I could tell her all about yer bonny lad," the nurse retorted with a sneer.

"Nothing's the matter with Roger," the girl said indignantly.

"It's not me ye've got t' convince."

"Well, then, Aunty's coming home in the morning, so I hope you're not planning to be away all night," Eva countered, bristling from the nurse's uncomfortable insinuation.

"Which is why I'll be back by midnight, ye ugly little brattle. G'night."

After the woman left, Eva tried to get back into Rosy's romance, but her argument with the nurse had put her out of temper and out of the mood for reading. Sighing, she thumped the volume shut and sat there drinking in the cool night air and the sound of the muffled surf and sea birds.

At length, Eva decided she might as well go to bed. Diligently, she locked the doors and windows to ensure her father could not leave the house. Then she ambled back to her room, burrowed under her covers, and soon fell fast asleep.

It was just eleven o' clock when Eva suddenly sat straight up in bed and glanced round. Something had brought her out of a sound slumber. Breathing quickly, she sat very still and listened.

Crreeak.

Eva's eyes shot over to her window—the one window she had forgotten to lock. To her horror, the glass frames were swinging outward on their hinges and groaning in protest.

Maybe the wind had shaken them open. Encouraged by this notion, the girl slid one foot out from under her blankets and rested her toes on the rug beside the bed. But instantly she drew her leg back, for two hands had emerged from outside the window and were gripping the sides of the frame. Soon, a dark shape surfaced and swallowed up the starlight peeping through the window.

In a frenzy of terror, Eva looked for some sort of weapon, but all she saw was a broken pencil and *Rosy Wilson's First Love*. These she snatched up and held in quivering hands as the shape in the window hoisted itself further in, landed on the floor with a muffled thump, and carefully closed the window again.

The poor girl wanted to scream so badly. But the scream that had rushed to her lips at the first sight of those dreadful hands was apparently just as terrified as she was, for it bolted right back down her throat and refused to come out again. Although she tried to get up and run, she felt as if someone had nailed her to her mattress; moving her legs now was impossible. Eva was trapped.

Meanwhile, the figure was slinking across the room toward her. She wished she had pretended to be asleep. She wished she had a knife or a gun or *something* damaging. She wished she had locked that window. For all that matter, she wished she wasn't alone in the first place!

With every creaking step, the intruder advanced upon her, until a tall masculine shadow was standing only inches from her bed. At that point, Eva decided she wanted to die, but she couldn't do that just then either.

"Well, hallo there," said the figure in a sweet, sinister, snakish hiss.

Eva could only sit holding that broken pencil and that silly romance novel. She imagined what Mrs. Abernathy would say when she found her body, still clutching *Rosy Wilson's First Love* as if it were the Bible.

"I thought you'd be asleep," the figure continued.

Eva moved her mouth, but that spineless scream refused to come forth. Her bed squeaked as the person sat down distressingly close to her.

"What's wrong, Eva?" said the intruder.

Then she recognized the voice; and she let out a sob. The novel and pencil fell from her hands, and the girl slumped trembling against a firm shoulder.

"Why, Eva, what's got into you?"

"I thought you were a burglar," Eva choked. "Thank God it's only you, Roger!"

"There, there, stop crying," the boy said, patting her soothingly. "Shhh, you'll wake up your father."

"I'm sorry!" Eva replied. "But what are you doing here? Why did you crawl through my window?"

"I didn't want to knock on the door," the boy explained. "You'd turn the light on, and then someone might see me."

"But through my window, Roger! You frightened me out of my mind!"

"I had to do it," he responded, lowering his voice. "Eva, where is your father?"

"Asleep on the sofa. Why do you ask?"

"That's lucky," Roger murmured, almost to himself. "We can get out without him seeing us."

"What are you talking about?" Eva asked with a start.

"Eva," Roger said, grasping her hands in his, "you've got to listen to me. You've got to come with me right now. You can't stay here any longer, not with him. Get a few things and come away with me this instant."

"You're teasing me! Whatever for?"

"I can't explain it all now," the boy returned irritably. "You'll have to take my word for it. You're not safe, but you'll be safe with me. I love you, Eva!" he continued in a voice taut with passion. "I can't take it anymore. You've just got to come away with me. We'll go off together, the two of us, and we won't tell anyone where we've gone. I have a friend in Yorkshire. You can stay with her until you're old enough, and then we can marry! And your father won't be able to touch you, then or ever! You'll be safe!"

"Good heavens, Roger!" Eva exclaimed, peeling her hands out of his grasp. "I am safe! Daddy's not going to hurt me. I don't know what's got into you!"

"The devil, Eva!" Roger swore, rising abruptly. "I said I love you!"

"I love you, too, Roger. I've told you that already. But this idea of running off in the middle of the night is insane! Why, Southdale's term ends next week; I've got exams on Monday! You're talking like a little boy or something, Roger! I don't understand you."

Eva reached over and turned on her nightstand lamp.

"Turn that off!" Roger growled and then did it himself.

"Roger!"

"You're coming with me and you're coming right now!" the boy demanded. "You're coming because you love me and you're not safe, and because I love you enough to make you happy and safe forever!"

"Roger, I *am* safe!"

"You're not!"

Roger's words came out with a shout this time, and he grabbed Eva's arm and yanked her out of bed. Eva couldn't see his face, but she could feel the muscles of his iron grip vibrating with rage.

"Come on!" he fumed.

"Roger, stop it! You're hurting me!" Eva cried, trying to twist herself free.

"No!" the boy barked. "I would never hurt you!"

"Then let go!"

In reply, Roger raised his free hand and struck her across the face.

Now Eva realized she was truly in danger.

"Right then," the boy panted, "come on!"

Eva glanced at her door, the only pathway of escape. It was just a little ajar.

"All right, Roger, I will," she consented, trying to sound calm. "Just please let me get a few things first. It's breezy tonight, and I'm only in my nightgown, you know."

"Of course," said the boy, his demeanor promptly returning to that sweet, pleasant manner Eva was used to. "Go right ahead, darling."

As he spoke, he let go of her arm. Immediately, the girl broke for the door. One moment, Eva had her fingers on the knob and could feel the door giving way under her grasp; the next, she was reeling backward, being dragged away by arms far stronger than she had ever imagined.

And finally, she screamed.

It was not a very loud scream. It was more like the gurgling shriek of sudden panic. Before Eva could let out a louder cry for help, Roger's hand clamped over her mouth.

"Now you stop it!" Roger seethed in her ear. "You stop it, or you'll be sorry!"

Eva struggled madly. He was dragging her to the window now, and she had a sickening feeling that if once Roger got her across that sill, she would never see her home again.

"I said stop it!" Roger yelled, shaking her. "I'm not going to hurt you!"

In response, the girl sank her teeth into his hand with all her might. Instantly, Roger shoved her forward and howled in pain. Slamming stomach-first into the side of her mattress, Eva tried to turn around and catch a breath to scream with; but the boy pushed her against the bed again in his fury.

"You little liar!" he howled, seizing her and drawing back his arm for another blow. "You ungrateful—"

Unexpectedly, Eva felt Roger's grasp around her tear away, sending her crumpling forward upon her bed. Clutching her stomach, she looked up and realized that someone else was in the room grappling with the boy.

She did not stay to see more. Fighting against her gelatinized legs and throbbing stomach, she rolled off the bed and stumbled out of the room. As she staggered down the hall, she could hear Roger roaring like an injured bear, and she expected to feel his arms around her any second.

As swiftly as she could, she whipped around the corner of the darkened hall and was just charging past the sitting room to the front door when she ran right into something barring her path.

"Let me go!" she squealed, fighting a pair of arms and hands. "Leave me alone!"

"Eva, what's going on?" the person cried.

For the second time, she recognized a voice that night, and for the second time she clutched the owner.

"Harold, help me!" she shrieked. "Save me! He's trying to kill me!"

Harold didn't need to ask what she was talking about. Even as Eva spoke, the boy heard Roger Wyatt's furious tones reverberating through the house.

"Go find a neighbor and get help!" Harold ordered, disentangling himself from her. "I'll stop him!"

Just then there came a crash and a long, clattering bang from Eva's room. Then there was silence.

The two children looked at one another, and Eva put her hand to her mouth.

"Stay here," Harold said grimly, "and if I shout, you run."

Leaving Eva in the semidarkness, the boy crept down the corridor. When he reached Eva's room, he put his hand inside, fumbled for the light switch on the wall, and prepared himself for what waited for him when the light came on.

Chapter 17

Click!

"Heaven help us," Harold breathed.

The place was in shambles. Eva's desk was turned over. Books, papers, lightbulb shards, and pillows were strewn everywhere. In the middle of the room, Roger Wyatt lay senseless upon the floor. Standing over him, breathing heavily and still holding the remains of the lamp with which he had struck the boy, was Eva's father.

"Harold?" Eva called shakily from the other room. "What happened? Is it all right?"

At the sound of Eva's voice, Ulysses turned around. For an instant, Harold thought he saw something like fury in the man's eyes; but the emotion rapidly evaporated, leaving Ulysses with an empty expression.

"Harold?" Eva yelled again. "Is it all right?"

Harold tried to think of how to respond to her, but he didn't know what to say. In the silence that followed, Eva pattered up the hall and stepped into the room.

When she saw Roger, she shrieked.

"Eva, don't look," Harold pleaded.

As the boy spoke, Ulysses swiftly pushed past him, caught Eva's arm, and dragged her out of the room.

Eva's mind was reeling as her father led her down the passage. So many things had happened so fast that she couldn't get her brain to process them all.

"Telephone the police!" Harold ordered, but his voice sounded funny and far-off.

The police. The police. There was a telephone in the hall.

"Wait, Daddy," Eva said, stopping by the machine and picking up the receiver. She wanted to dial, but her father would not let go of her arm.

"Cot's Haven constabulary," the girl said to the operator.

Before an officer could answer, Eva started to cry.

"Hallo? Hallo?" a voice said on the other end of the line.

"Here, let me handle it," Harold offered, turning up unexpectedly and taking the receiver.

Eva allowed herself to be led into the sitting room. It did not look like their sitting room. To her, it was unfamiliar and murky, as if it were leagues under the ocean.

Lightly, Ulysses pushed her onto the sofa and let go of her arm.

"Daddy?" Eva murmured, looking up. "Daddy, it was you who saved me! You must have heard me scream. You *heard* me! Roger was right. Oh, no. Harold!" she shouted. "Harold, where's Roger? Is he dead? Harold!"

Harold sprinted into the room.

"Sit down, sit down!" he urged.

"He went insane!" Eva panted. "I couldn't understand! He tried to hurt me! Is he dead? Please tell me he isn't dead! Daddy didn't kill him, did he?"

"He's alive," Harold replied. "But he's been knocked clean out. The police are bringing the doctor with them."

When Dr. McCabe arrived, he glanced at Eva and then

went straight to her room. But Chief Constable Holt, a tall and stocky fellow in his sixties, had several things to say to Eva. After looking round her room and talking to the doctor, he returned and started asking questions.

Eva did her best to answer and recounted everything she had personally experienced, but her story did not satisfy the man. He persisted in questioning her about what happened between Roger Wyatt and her father that night and wasn't pleased to hear she knew nothing about it.

Harold York had little to add to the matter. Since his parents were visiting his uncle in Eastbourne, the lad had decided to take a long stroll along the cliffs that night. Passing the Starbucks' back garden, he was surprised to hear loud, threatening voices issuing from the house. Desperate, he tried to get in by the back door, and then the front, until he finally broke through a window in the sitting room.

The lad was in the middle of explaining what he had done after he met Eva in the hall when the doctor came back.

"I've called for an ambulance," McCabe declared. "Someone should probably contact young Wyatt's parents and meet them at the hospital."

"How is he?" the chief constable asked.

"He is unconscious now, and I'm sure he will have a beastly headache when he awakes. But he's strong. I think he'll come out of it nicely in the end. How do you feel?" the doctor inquired, turning to the girl.

"I'm all right, I guess," Eva replied. "My face and stomach hurt a bit."

"Too be expected," McCabe muttered, bending down and examining the bruise forming on her cheek. "But hallo, you're bleeding!"

"I am? Where?"

"Here on your shoulder. See, it goes down the back of your sleeve."

"But it doesn't hurt," Eva remarked, looking at her arm.

"Nor should it; this isn't your blood," McCabe revealed, rolling up her sleeve.

"Did you touch the Wyatt boy after he'd been hit?" said Constable Holt.

"Oh, no, not at all. They wouldn't let me near him."

"Well, surely you must have," the policeman argued. "How else can you explain it?"

"Did your father touch you?" the doctor asked.

"Yes, he pulled me away."

"Well, that explains it, then," Harold stated. "Mr. Starbuck fought with Wyatt and then grabbed Eva."

"Where is your father, anyway?" Holt questioned.

Eva glanced around the room.

"Why, he must have left while we were talking!"

"Oh, did he? Well, he won't get far. I've got a man outside each door."

"Daddy wouldn't run away like that!" Eva contended indignantly. "He hasn't done anything wrong, anyway."

"We'll see about that."

Dr. McCabe, who had left a few moments before, now stepped into the room.

"I think you should be looking for a large knife, Constable," he said.

"A knife? What for?"

"Because I have just found Ulysses Starbuck fainted at the back of the hall, with a knife wound in his arm."

161

It was half-past twelve and the police and doctor (and Harold, after some persuasion) had finally gone. Mrs. Abernathy had returned not long ago, complaining that it was all Eva's fault that Roger had hurt Ulysses, and now the man would be in bed for weeks and probably never use his arm again. To be fair, the doctor predicted something entirely different, but the nurse shunned his sunny prognosis completely.

Poor Eva had nothing to say to the Scotswoman's accusations. For one thing, she partially believed them, and for another she was emotionally and physically exhausted. But she didn't want to sleep in her room again after what happened that night. She didn't want to sleep at all. So, taking a blanket from her bed, Eva wrapped herself up and sat on the sofa.

She had not been there more than half an hour when there was a step in the hall and her father walked into the room.

"You're supposed to be in bed, Daddy," she said.

But he sat down in his usual place. Scooting closer to him, Eva put out her hand and touched his arm.

"Daddy, I thought you had come back tonight," she murmured. "It was so wonderful. *You* were wonderful. I wish you hadn't hurt Roger that badly, but I know you didn't mean it. You were just trying to protect me, weren't you?"

Ulysses' eyes began to close, and his head leaned forward onto his breast.

"I don't know if you can hear me. I don't suppose you can right now. The doctor says tonight was a passing incident, like last year when you recognized Mr. Euston. I wish it weren't true, because it was so nice for you to hold my arm like that.

"I've been such a fool!" she moaned, shaking her head. "Mrs. Abernathy is right: this is all my fault. If I'd just listened to Harold, this never would have happened. I knew he was right, even if I didn't want to believe it. Oh, I just can't talk about it any longer. I can't even think about it. I just wish none of this ever happened. I wish I were six again, Daddy, and that you hadn't gone to war yet."

Eva leaned over and wrapped her arms around his neck, the way she used to when she was very little. It did not feel the same now, but she was so empty inside that she held on anyway.

"He reminded me of you," she whispered into her father's ear. "At least I thought he did. I thought he was so much like you that it could almost be the same, but in another way. I know that doesn't make any sense. And you probably can't hear me anyway, Daddy. But I'm sorry. Please, I'm so sorry!"

She ended by crying silently into his shoulder.

Eva must have fallen asleep that way, clinging to her father in the dark; because when they found her early in the morning, she was still holding on to him. And he, with his one uninjured arm, was holding on to her.

When Eva awoke, she was not on the sofa. The window beside her was open, and a warm summer breeze was blowing the blue curtains apart and sending flashes of light onto the olive wall across the room. Sitting up, Eva realized she was in her father's bed and dressed in a fresh nightgown with her hair tied behind her head. Ulysses was lying next to her, still asleep.

She glanced at the clock on the mantle: it was a quarter to eleven. Yawning, she put on her robe, which she found draped neatly over a chair, and crept out of the room. When she got into the hall, the first thing she noticed was happy voices coming from the kitchen. One sounded like her aunt's, but the other appeared new to her. Sneaking down the hall, Eva poked her head shyly through the kitchen door.

"Why, Eva!" Agnes exclaimed.

Her aunt looked wonderful. Her eyes were dancing, her face was blushed from just a little too much sun, her dress was springy and light, her hair was down, and her make-up was strikingly vibrant. All this Eva noted in an instant, for Agnes hurried over and trapped her niece in a hug.

"Darling, we're so glad you're safe!" her aunt said, squeezing her tighter than Eva anticipated. "How are you? Are you feeling better this morning? Did you sleep well? Does anything hurt?"

"I'm fine, thank you," Eva replied, smiling and looking with a little bewilderment at the man sitting at the table.

Agnes followed her niece's gaze.

"Eva, you remember Mr. Euston, don't you?" she asked.

"Yes, it's nice to see you again, sir."

Morton Euston, beaming like a lighthouse and rather more tanned than Eva remembered him, rose from his seat.

"Hey again, Eva!" he said cheerily. "I'm glad you're safe and sound."

"Have you come to visit Daddy again?"

"Well, actually I'm—"

"Oh, shush!" Agnes interrupted. "Just a moment! Here Eva, sit down. Are you comfortable? Good. Now, I've got something to tell you. Did you notice that I was getting letters rather often in the past several months?"

"You mean the ones from Portsmouth?" Eva asked. "I only noticed that a while ago."

"Portsmouth, darling?"

"Weren't they from Portsmouth?"

"No, dear. I think one was, but that was only Major Arnold asking after Ulysses. What I'm trying to tell you is that Mr. Euston and I have been conversing for some time."

"Since last year," Euston inserted.

"Yes, well, it started with things about your father, but it gradually—well, a couple weeks ago it all came to a head, and I went down to Portsmouth to meet him coming in from America," Agnes continued.

"And we got married the next day," Mort Euston finished proudly.

Eva's eyes grew two sizes.

"No!" she gasped.

"Yes!" Agnes grinned.

"You're actually—after all—I thought—Aunty, congratulations!" Eva burbled, hugging her aunt again.

"I know it's a bit of a shock for you, darling."

"No," Eva laughed. "I mean yes. I thought it was someone else! But I've never seen you so happy, Aunty!"

"I haven't been this happy, dear," Agnes smiled, "not in a very long time."

"Are we moving to America, then?"

"No, we're staying here, at least for now. Mort has taken an engineering position in Eastbourne."

"Oh, Aunty, Daddy would be so happy for you. I only wish he knew."

"He might someday," Euston said. "You never know."

"Does this mean we can sack Mrs. Abernathy?" Eva asked expectantly.

"No, not yet, darling," Agnes shook her head. "I'll be at the factory awhile longer, and we need someone experienced to take care of your father right now."

"But Aunty, we don't need a nurse anymore. And Mrs. Abernathy is so horrid. She's gone out twice and left us alone at night. She did last night, when—"

Eva shuddered and said no more.

"We'll talk about last night when you're feeling better about it," her aunt said. "And you've just got to trust me about Mrs.

Abernathy. I know she's rude, and we will address that when she returns from the village. But she's so devoted to your father that I want to keep her if possible."

The girl frowned.

"Now, cheer up, dear," Agnes said, raising the girl's chin. "Why don't you go and dress now? In a little while, we'll all four have a picnic in the garden. Does that sound nice?"

Eva thought about how long it had been since the Starbucks had picnicked anywhere.

"Nice?" she answered. "Oh, no. It sounds lovely."

For some time, Agnes had been lost in a dream world. Oh, she had tended to her responsibilities during that period; but now that she was back home, those duties leapt up and demanded attention in earnest. First there was Mrs. Abernathy: she was stubborn. And she was not at all happy that Mr. Euston had arrived. After being firmly reprimanded by him for abandoning Eva and Ulysses, she almost left her position altogether before deciding she would stay for her patient's sake.

Amidst this little drama there was Eva, who had been running about with a dangerous boy for months without her aunt's knowledge. Agnes had never talked to Eva about boys. A woman who avoids the idea of marriage or romance as a painful memory is often not apt to discuss the subject with others. The fact was, she had no idea what to say to Eva about what happened with Roger. In the end, it was all so uncomfortable that she didn't even try.

But worst of all there was something else. And that something telephoned one day and asked for an appointment.

"This has been a most unusual situation," Constable Holt admitted after motioning Agnes into a chair in front of his desk.

"In my twenty years of experience, I've never come into anything like it. It's certainly not a thing that's happened in Cot's Haven before."

"You mean the Wyatt boy attacking Eva?" Agnes asked.

"Well, yes," the man said, "and no. The fact is the boy is rather out of my scope. He's been taken to a different hospital and gone under special observation and such. I can't say anything more about him. There's people higher up that's taking care of his situation. It's not the boy that we've got to worry about now."

"Oh?"

"You see, his parents are blaming this whole affair on your brother."

"My brother!"

"Yes, I'm afraid to say it," Holt confessed. "There's an accusation about previous provocation on Mr. Starbuck's part. And while I can't say I believe that myself, I still have to consider him striking the boy with a lamp and doing him a great deal of harm."

"The boy attacked my niece and came at Ulysses with a filleting knife!" Agnes returned angrily. "How did they expect my brother to react?"

"Roger Wyatt claims he was defending himself and only drew the knife after Mr. Starbuck struck him the first time," the constable explained.

"First time?"

"He did it three times, you know."

Agnes leaned back in her chair.

"I didn't know that," she breathed.

"At any rate, we understand that Mr. Starbuck was not—is not—he can't really be held accountable for his actions in his current—state," Holt said, choosing his words with difficulty. "I knew him well enough myself to be thoroughly convinced that he never would have reacted so excessively in the past."

"Never," Agnes asserted.

"But we do have the present problem to consider, you know," the man went on. "I've talked with the magistrate, and he's willing to dismiss this part of the matter on one condition."

"Which is?"

"If your brother becomes violent or disruptive or anything like it again, he should be moved to an institution. Now, I understand your feelings on this, but you must look at things from my position. I've got the village's safety on my shoulders, I do. It may never happen again, but if it does, I can't leave it be. It was all I could do to convince the magistrate to let things pass this time, you know."

As soon as the chief constable had uttered the word *institution*, Agnes stopped hearing him. Every bit of her concentration was channeled to keeping herself from pure panic. She could hardly believe it. This could not be happening. She would not let it happen, not again—never, never, never again.

"Miss?"

Agnes blinked.

"Eh, yes?" she stuttered.

"I was just saying I hope you understand," Holt informed her.

"Ah, yes, I do. Thank you."

"I'm dreadful sorry about all this, you know. It's not a nice business at all."

"Thank you," Agnes said, rising stiffly.

"Then this Friday at one o' clock is convenient for the appointment with the psychiatrist?"

"Psychiatrist!"

"Yes, it's just routine," the constable assured her. "Part of the orders from the Arm—from the magistrate. They only want to see how he is, you know."

Agnes swallowed hard.

"Oh," she replied at length. "Where again?"

"Portsmouth Military Hospital."

"The military hospital?"

"Yes, well, it's more convenient that way," Holt explained promptly. "The same doctors and such."

Eva's aunt turned to leave.

"I really am sorry," said the policeman.

But Agnes did not hear him. The only thing she heard as she left the man's office was the word *institution* repeating over and over, like the perpetual gongs of a funeral bell.

<hr/>

"Hey," Euston said, poking his head through the doorway.

"Don't do that!" the nurse gasped, turning round angrily.

"Sorry, I just wanted to see the sergeant," Euston replied, stepping into Ulysses' room.

"Knock then! Can't ye see I'm dressin' his wound?"

"Well, here, let me help you," Euston suggested, stepping over to the desk and picking up a bottle of iodine.

When Euston approached, Ulysses, who sat in a chair beside the desk, gave a start and gripped the arms of the chair.

"Whoa, Sergeant, it's okay," said the other man. "It's just Mort Euston."

"I can do this myself," the nurse growled, snatching the bottle from Euston. "Ye should go. Yer upsettin' him."

"It's okay, Sergeant," Euston went on, bending down to Ulysses' level and gently putting a hand on his shoulder. "Why, you're shaking. What's wrong?"

"Yer the problem," snapped the nurse.

Euston stared intently at his old sergeant. Ulysses' eyes were still distant and unseeing, but the expression on his face was one of growing panic. He was breathing rapidly. And he was sweating.

"He was like this before I came in," Euston said, turning to the nurse.

"His arm hurts. It frightens him," the lady replied, tearing a bandage. "I don't suppose ye'd understand that."

"No, I do," murmured Euston, sitting down on a stool beside Ulysses. "Here, Sergeant, give me your hand. I know what he's thinking, because I was there," he added to the nurse. "And if you don't mind, I'm going to stay there with him until you're done."

Chapter 18

It was a lucky thing that the holidays were upon Eva. The thought of going to Southdale School every day, when the corridors would be ringing with the news of Roger Wyatt (in various stages of grapevine growth), was nauseating to Eva. Doggedly, she made herself go to school that Monday and Tuesday. She didn't talk to anyone. She took her exams and went home. By Wednesday, the term was over, and Eva was praying that the six-week summer holiday would turn Roger Wyatt into old news for her schoolmates.

In the meantime, the *Crier* was simply screaming the news of the attack. Wars, affairs of state, and far-off discoveries were all right in their own way, but the folk of Cot's Haven much preferred a local drama. Not even the sudden marriage of Agnes Starbuck to a peculiar American was enough to distract people from the excitement of a real, honest row in the village. After months of being old news, Ulysses Starbuck was again a topic of keen interest in Cot's Haven; but the things that were being said about him were no longer so complimentary or admirable.

"Did you hear the Wyatts are moving away?" Mandy

Butterfield asked one afternoon after she met Priscilla leaving the hairdressers.

"Yes, I did hear something about that," Priscilla replied, adjusting a lock of newly curled hair.

"Honestly, I think it's rather lucky," Mandy went on, linking arms with her friend as they walked along the street. "That Roger Wyatt is a real bad apple, you know. He's touched in the head, I'd say. Why, just think what he might have done to Eva if Mr. Starbuck hadn't stopped him!"

"Of course, we only have Eva's word that Roger ever did try to hurt her," Priscilla noted with a modest smile. "It's rather interesting that everyone takes it for granted that things happened the way our dear friend said."

"Why, Priscilla!" Mandy reprimanded. "You know Eva wouldn't lie!"

"Now, now, darling," Priscilla returned, patting the other girl's arm, "I never said such a thing. I only think it's interesting, that's all. Of course, I didn't know Roger Wyatt too well, but I always believed him to be a charming, gentle sort. So has everyone else. Don't you think it might be far more likely that things happened the way Roger's parents say they did, with Eva getting just a bit hysterical and misunderstanding something Roger said or did? And then Mr. Starbuck would have attacked the poor boy without any real provocation."

"Well, I don't really think so," Mandy replied meekly. "For one thing, Eva doesn't get hysterical. And then, Mr. Starbuck was always so kind and gentle when I knew him."

"Ah, but you must remember that he's feeble-minded now," Priscilla shook her head. "A man of that sort is capable of almost anything, you know, even if he didn't used to be."

"Really?" Mandy wondered, her large blue eyes growing even

larger and bluer. "Oh, dear, but wouldn't that make him rather dangerous?"

"Certainly, darling. Why, you see already what he's done to poor Roger! People in that condition could go off at any time."

"Oh, my!" cried Mandy. "But shouldn't we warn Eva?"

"Oh, she's all right," said Priscilla. "He won't hurt *her*, or any of his other family. Those people don't do that sort of thing. It's only everyone else that's in danger. That's what Father says. I shouldn't go over there often if I were you, dear. It's really not safe.

"Well!" she finished, unhooking her arm from her friend's. "I've got to run home in time for tea. I'll see you later, Mandy darling!"

Mandy Butterfield had planned on dropping by to see Eva that day. But instead, she went straight home to her family's sheep farm, where, as far as she knew, she was safe.

◞◠

Roger Wyatt groaned. His whole head ached and throbbed like a gate under the buffet of a battering ram. For the past two hours, his head had been pounding relentlessly and robbing sleep from him. Wearily, he turned over onto his other side. That was when he saw the military officer sitting by his bed.

"Who are you?" the boy demanded. 'What do you want?"

"I want to talk."

"What time is it?"

"Half past nine. It's a fine night."

"Are you another doctor?"

"No, I am not."

"I don't want to talk to anyone," Roger said sullenly.

"That I have already gathered from the reports. You've been

most uncooperative. The psychiatrist can't find a single reason for your actions a couple weeks ago."

"Maybe I didn't have one."

"Maybe you did," the officer returned. "You know, the British Army discovered something rather interesting recently. We discovered that a certain Marvin Selkirk was still alive. Rather unfortunately, it took us some time to come upon this information. But I have a feeling you tied those ends together long ago."

Roger did not reply.

"Since you are not inclined to tell me anything about this," the officer continued, "allow me. Your real name is Roger Short. Your elder brother was Marvin Short. Both your parents died when you were quite young. Having no other relatives, you were sent to an orphanage."

"They didn't die that way," Roger broke in.

"What way?"

"The way you said it: 'both your parents died,' and that's all. My mother died when I was born, and my father couldn't stand the grief and shot himself when I was three. I was in the room when he did it. So was my brother. He shot himself right in front of us. That's the way they died. They didn't just die."

There was silence for a moment as Roger struggled to master his emotions again.

"Are you going to finish this?" the officer questioned.

The boy shook his head.

"Well, then I will," the man replied. "By a nasty trick of fate, you were adopted by the Wyatt family, but your brother remained at the orphanage for several years."

"No one wanted him. He was too old," huffed the boy.

"Then he got out and joined the British Army in 1942. He wrote you often enough through that year, but somewhere in '43 the letters just stopped. Your adoptive parents weren't interested in your brother, so you made inquiries on your own. The only thing you could learn was that he was missing in action. And so he was for the next two years, until you discovered at the end of the war that your brother had been captured, sent to Das Grab, successfully escaped, and at last returned to England.

"But where was he, eh? No calls, no letters, no visits. Not like him at all, I suppose."

Roger nodded.

"Then, sooner or later, you happened to move to Cot's Haven and make the acquaintance of Eva Starbuck. She innocently told you that her father had escaped Das Grab with a Marvin Short. But the Marvin Short she described wasn't anything like your brother. Your brother's hair was blonde, and this man's was black. This Marvin Short was apparently at least five years older than you brother, too. I'm sure it didn't take long for you to realize that your brother's absent letters and visits and his sudden change in traits simply reeked of imposter.

"Now I am a fair judge of character," the officer said, crossing his arms and looking closely at the boy. "I suspect you did a bit of digging and found out where this fellow lived. By the time you got to him in early June, he was like as badly off as we later found him. If he happened to be drunk, it was probably easy to twist the truth out of him."

Roger laughed.

"Three sheets to the wind, he was," the boy revealed. "Thought I was Marvin and came apart right then and there."

"And I think a smart lad like you realized that, while you had Selkirk in your power, you'd only be bagging a cub and not the lion. What you really wanted was the author of the plot to kill your brother. What you really wanted was Starbuck."

Roger clenched his fists and closed his eyes.

"He killed my brother," he hissed. "Killed him as sure as if he'd been a Jerry and murdered him himself. Killed my only brother, my only family, the only person I ever cared about!"

"So, you decided to get even," the officer interrupted. "You decided that you would take away the person *he* cared about the most. Kill her, just as he killed your brother."

"No!" Roger defended, trying to sit up and then falling back again with the pain of it. "It wasn't that way! I didn't hate Eva! I wouldn't kill her! I wouldn't touch a hair on her head."

"Just strike her and kick the air out of her."

"But I didn't want to!" Roger maintained. "I had to! I was trying to save her. He didn't deserve her, so I was going to take her away from him. She would have been safe with me. Only she didn't want to go. I had to convince her somehow! I loved her, and I thought she loved me. Don't you see, I only wanted to get her away from him? The poor girl didn't know what he was like. I didn't blame her for Marvin's death!"

"Then you just brought along that knife to whittle with, eh?"

"I was going to trip the catch on the window," Roger answered. "Look here, I haven't done anything wrong. If I harmed Starbuck, well, I was only protecting myself, and he deserves far worse. I wasn't the one who attacked him. He attacked *me*. It's him you should be going after. He hurt me and he killed my brother, and by heaven he needs his comeuppance! Someone should give it to him!"

"I daresay someone will," the officer replied, rising and taking his hat from the bedside table. "I also dare to say there's nothing wrong in your attic, though it may take the doctors a bit to come round to that truth. I'll recommend your being taken to a civilian hospital to finish your recovery; there's no more information we need from you."

"Then you believe me?" Roger queried. "You believe I didn't hate Eva, and I didn't set out to harm the old man?"

"I believe you didn't hate the young lady," said the officer. "But whatever you think, I find it highly unlikely that you loved her. But that is none of my affair. As far as setting out to kill Ulysses Starbuck, well, what I think doesn't matter. You're safe, you know: no one can prove what you really meant to do. But I suppose if you did want to harm him, you too, lad, will get you own comeuppance in time."

❦

"Mind if I come in?"

Eva leaned back against the headboard of her bed and set down her book.

"Sure," she said, smiling at her uncle.

Mr. Euston walked into Eva's room with that unconventional, broad gait of a self-made man who is used to having a lot of space about him.

"Feel okay being in here again?" he asked, sticking his tawny hands into his pockets and looking round the room.

"It's all right," Eva replied, "as long as I leave the door open at night."

"Are *you* all right?"

Eva stared at the man.

"I'm fine, thank you," she said eventually.

"You don't have to tell me," her uncle returned with a shrug. "I know I'm still a stranger to you. I'm probably a pretty strange stranger, too. That's okay. We'll be friends soon, I think. Anyway—"

Eva did not listen to the rest. She had been watching him, and, as he stood there talking, he seemed like old open-faced Harold speaking out his mind. And then he looked like her father when he was sweet and strong and trying to comfort her. Before Euston could finish, the girl's eyes brimmed over with tears.

"Whoa, what did I say?" Euston asked in alarm.

"Nothing," Eva shook her head, slapping away the tears. "Nothing, it's nothing."

"Well, that settles it. You're definitely not okay," Euston observed, sitting down at the foot of the bed where her father had sat so many years ago. "Is it this mental hospital business?"

Not knowing how to express what else was troubling her, Eva bobbed her head.

"Well, I know you and Agnes are worried about it, but I really don't think we have to. Ulysses has never done something like that before, and there's no reason why he should do it again. It's not like he woke up one morning and flew off the handle. Something big happened to set him off."

"And it's my fault that it did!" Eva replied despairingly. "And what if that makes him—I don't know how to say it—go off more easily? What if something small happens tonight or tomorrow or next week, and he hurts someone again? That would be my fault. And it would be my fault if they put Daddy away in an institution for the rest of his life. And it's my fault that Aunty's been so worried lately, and that the Wyatts are going away, and that Harold probably will never forgive me for not listening to him. It's just all because of me!" Eva concluded, tucking her knees to her chest and hiding her face behind them.

She sat that way for a few minutes. Finally, the room became so still that she looked up to see if Euston had left. But he was still sitting on the edge of her bed. When her head came up, he smiled kindly.

"You know, none of that was true," he said. "None of it. Hear?"

"Bed in five minutes!" Agnes called from across the hall.
Euston stood up.

"Did you say good night to your aunt?" he questioned.

"Not yet."

"Then how 'bout you give me a hug, and I'll pass it along?"

Eva reached up and hugged her uncle. She held on a little longer than she meant to, for she was thinking about hugging her father.

"None of it," he finished when she let go. "Got it?"

"Yes. Good night, Uncle Morton."

"Night, sweetheart," he said, and put out the light.

Sweetheart. Eva turned over with her face to the wall and wrapped her arms around one of her pillows. Weeks ago, she had wondered if having an uncle were anything like having a father. Now she knew the answer: it was nothing like it. Mr. Euston was a nice man, but all he was and all he could ever be was a reminder of what it had been like to have her daddy.

Eva squeezed the pillow tighter. Her chest ached. It ached like an empty, empty cavern. And it felt like nothing could ever make it stop aching.

The next day, Eva was so lonely and sad that she decided she would rather be with her friend Mandy again than hold her grudge about Brighton and Priscilla. But when she called Mandy to invite her over, her friend complained that she had so many things to do and could not find the time. Feeling worse than before, Eva set down the phone and slinked out into the back garden to sit on the stone bench. She thought about finding Harold, but she felt so guilty for how splendid he had been despite her recent animosity that she supposed she was unworthy of his company today.

The bench was too hot to sit on. But she sat on it anyway.

Then it started to rain. But she sat in it anyway. She had probably been drenching herself for a good ten minutes when a rattling crash startled her out of her sorrows. Jumping up, she splashed out of the garden and into the house.

"Mrs. Abernathy," she shouted, "what was that?"

Another bang issued from the other side of the house.

"Mrs. Abernathy!"

"Aye!" the nurse yelled, clattering into the kitchen with a red face and a very bizarre expression.

"I heard something fall," Eva said. "What was it?"

"I dropped somethin'," the lady snapped. "What are ye doin' here?"

"What do you mean?"

"I thought ye'd gone into the village."

"No, I was just in the garden."

"Well, tell me next time, ye little brat!" the nurse shot back with sudden ferocity.

"What does it matter to you?" Eva wondered, astonished by the lady's demeanor.

"It doesn't!" Mrs. Abernathy retorted. "I'm cleanin', that's all. I don't like ye underfoot when I'm cleanin'."

"Well, then I'll just change my dress and go into the village," Eva replied, more hurt than angry.

"No, ye'll jest go no'," the nurse insisted, pushing Eva to the door.

"I'm soaking wet!"

"The sun's out. Ye'll be dry soon enough."

"I won't!" Eva protested.

But it was useless. Mrs. Abernathy had already shoved her outside and locked the door behind her.

Eva was gone about four hours. There was a cartoon playing at the Telescope, so she went and saw that. Afterward, she cycled around the countryside for the afternoon. When she got home, tired and hungry, it was close to four o' clock.

Since her aunt and uncle wouldn't be home for dinner for at least two hours, Eva went into the kitchen and started preparing herself a sandwich. She was just cutting some lettuce when she had a curious feeling.

Something was wrong.

Pausing with a knife in one hand and a head of lettuce in the other, Eva stood and listened. But the house was perfectly still. There was not a single sound to be alarmed by.

Or maybe that was the thing that was so alarming.

"Mrs. Abernathy?" she called.

Silence.

"Daddy?"

Still nothing.

Maybe they had gone somewhere. Eva looked over at the icebox for a note; but there was nothing.

"Well, is anyone home?" she shouted.

When again there was no reply, Eva decided Mrs. Abernathy was definitely not at home. Angrily suspecting that the nurse had gone off again and left her father, Eva tromped out of the kitchen and into the sitting room.

Ulysses was not there.

"Must be in bed," she decided, and she went to look in his room.

Her father's bed was empty, and unmade.

Now Eva was getting worried. Swiftly, she went around the house, checking in all the rooms for her father. Then she checked them again. Then she made sure he wasn't following her as he had once before.

But this time, he was really gone.

Maybe Mrs. Abernathy had taken him with her. But what if she had not? What if, in the nurse's absence, Ulysses had wandered out of the house?

"Daddy!" Eva exploded, galloping from room to room. "Daddy, where are you?"

She checked every room a third time, praying fervently that she had missed something. And then when she went into her father's room, she found she had.

The window was open. It was wide open. Her stomach tossing, Eva stumbled over to the sill and peered outside. The azalea bush under the window was half-crushed, and on one side of it were bare footprints in the rain-softened earth. The footprints were leading away from the house.

"Oh, no," Eva breathed. "Oh, no, no."

Mrs. Abernathy would pay for this. This was all her fault.

Eva glanced down at the rug next to the window. Smudged into the cream-colored fibers was another footprint. But this one was red. Eva whirled and saw that there were more prints. Feeling sick, the girl followed the tracks out into the hall until they reached the bathroom. Holding her breath, Eva looked in.

She had just glanced into that little room before. It was so small, and she had not really expected to find him there. Now that she really looked, she wondered how she could have missed what lay before her.

There were bottles, a razor, pieces of rope, and other paraphernalia spilled or broken on the floor. A wooden kitchen chair was lying turned over in the clutter. And little dark red spots were everywhere.

Then there was the bathtub. She had never bothered to look in there.

She stepped forward and drew back the curtain that concealed the tub. In seconds, she was bent over the toilet throwing up. Finally, when her stomach was empty, she staggered out of the bathroom and made for the telephone.

She dialed numbers without seeing them; all she could see was what was in that tub.

"Yorks," said a voice.

"Harold?"

"Hallo, Eva!" came his merry, reassuring tone. "What is it?"

"Harold, can you come over?" she inquired in a voice devoid of emotion.

"Right away. Eva, is there something the matter?"

"Harold," Eva murmured, "Mrs. Abernathy is dead."

Chapter 19

In fifteen minutes, both Harold and his father were at the front door. Eva opened it mechanically and said only three words: "In the bathroom."

Patrick York jogged down the hall without asking any questions. He was only gone a minute.

"She is dead, isn't she?" Eva asked when Mr. York came into the sitting room.

"She is," said Patrick. "Eva, how did it happen?"

"I don't know," the girl replied. "I wasn't there. I came home and I thought everyone was gone. Daddy wasn't here. He's still not here!"

"Be quiet for a bit, dear," Mr. York instructed. "Harold, stay with her. I'll be back shortly."

Eva heard him go into the kitchen and pick up the wall telephone.

"What's he doing, Harold?"

"I think he's calling the constable."

"Does he have to?"

"I think so, Eva."

"Well," she mumbled, "I suppose he should then. Harold?"

"Yes, Eva?"

"Harold, Daddy killed her."

"Eva," Harold said gently. "It might have been an accident."

Eva gaped at him. Obviously, Harold had not seen Mrs. Abernathy in that bathtub. Eva had. She knew it could not possibly have been an accident.

When Chief Constable Holt told Agnes what happened, she did not cry, or gasp, or even appear shocked. She took it all so beautifully and bravely that the constable could scarce believe it. She merely called her husband and told him to come home straight away. Then, seeing that the house and neighborhood were crawling with policemen being ordered about by an inspector form the county seat, she asked if Eva could stay with the Butterfields that night. Holt agreed, and soon Agnes was driving her niece out into the countryside.

"I'm sorry," Eva offered from the passenger seat of the car.

"For what?"

"For leaving. It wouldn't have happened if I had been there. He wouldn't have done that."

"Eva, I'm only glad you weren't there."

They drove along in silence for several more minutes before Eva spoke again.

"I'm sorry."

"Why?"

"Because I'm to blame."

"No, you're not," said her aunt flatly.

Another few minutes passed.

"I'm sorry for not being brave," Eva sniffed. "I've really tried not to cry, but I just can't keep it back any longer. It was so awful, and I'm so scared, Aunty! Mrs. Abernathy is dead! Where is Daddy? What are they going to do when they find him? Are they going to kill him? Did he know what he did? Aunty, I can't stop crying!" the child burbled.

"Yes, you can."

"I—I—I—c—can't!"

"Stop it!" Agnes shouted.

The surprise of her aunt's vehement command shocked the sobs right out of Eva and left her whimpering and hiccupping.

When they reached the Butterfield farm, Agnes let Eva out of the car without a word and drove straight home. After she arrived, her husband was waiting for her on the steps; but she said nothing to him. She did not even want him to touch her.

Within an hour, all the police but a couple constables patrolling the neighborhood had gone away for the night. And it was then, when the house was quiet and private, that Agnes accepted her husband's strong hand and let the tears come.

And for a long time, not even Agnes Euston could stop crying.

∽っ

"I blame myself, Major," said Chief Constable Halsted Holt.

He was leaning back smoking in his office chair at the constabulary, and to be honest, he didn't appear very guilty about anything.

"I saw it coming, you know," he continued after another puff of his cigar. "But I didn't want to believe it. Should have spent my time convincing the magistrate to have Starbuck committed instead of trying to get him free. And now, of course, you tell me that things are even worse than I thought, that the Army wants him, too, for an even worse crime. It's despicable! I saw it coming and I didn't stop it!"

"Remember I told you that in confidence," Major Arnold commented, "and only to let you know what your men might be up against. No other civilian knows about it just now. We'd like to keep it that way for the present."

"Ah, so you did, and you will," the constable affirmed. "I'll keep it mum, to be sure. But it's a ghastly business, isn't it? You saw the way poor Abernathy broke down when he saw the lady in the morgue. Lucky thing he didn't see her *before* then. She was a sight in that tub, with the blood and all. I never saw so much of it. Of course, Inspector Downes says it's only because I haven't seen many murders in my years at the constabulary; but I was in the Great War, mind, and I saw my share of death. As I said, it was quite a sight, it was."

"The inspector is convinced it was murder, then?" Arnold asked.

"He is, and so am I. What else could it have been? A man may slip in a tub and knock his head on the waterspout when he's bathing, but he don't get in a dry tub in all his clothes and do it."

"The daughter said the woman was cleaning when she saw her last," Arnold observed.

"Well, I don't know about your missus, if you've got one, but my missus don't climb into the tub to clean it," chuckled the constable. "And I might add she wasn't dressed to clean when we found her; and there wasn't a scrub nor bottle of vinegar in sight. No, sir, I think we'd be balmy if we concluded anything but that the woman was murdered."

"How does the inspector explain the footprints on the rug?" Arnold questioned, undaunted by the constable's remarks.

"Well, the blood's hers, you know," the constable replied with some surprise.

"And what was on the walls, too, I expect?"

"Why, naturally! I don't know what your point is. It only means we've got more evidence."

"You're right indeed," the major muttered, rubbing his chin

thoughtfully. "There was a great deal of evidence around, wasn't there?"

"Anyway, we'll get him soon enough," Holt went on, gesturing with his cigar at a map of the countryside tacked behind him on the wall. "A chap can't hide for long in these parts, you know. It's all open country and bare cliffs, and a mere handful of copses about. And then the man is half-witted at best, according to Dr. McCabe and that psychiatrist's report you brought along. By the way, it was clever of you having Starbuck examined that way. Now we have a real expert's opinion to go by."

"It was a sensible maneuver," said the major. "It's important to know whether we're dealing with a feeble-minded man or a clever liar."

"Well, at any rate, his being half-witted should make him easier to find," the constable concluded. "Between the inspector's and my men, we'll have him in no time."

"Alive, if possible."

"Of course! In forty-eight hours, he'll be struggling and kicking in one of those cells down the hall, I assure you."

"I hope you're right," said the major, "because if it's any longer than forty-eight hours, I don't think you'll find him alive."

Twenty-four tiresome hours of searching passed, but a new rain-streaked day arrived without a sign of Ulysses Starbuck. The village was frightened: a madman was loose, and there was no telling where he would go next. Doors were locked, dogs were tied to gates, and children went nowhere without their parents. By the time the fated forty-eight hours had passed, the little Cot's Haven constabulary had been swamped with complaints and false leads from overly imaginative citizens. Yet they had still not captured their man.

"And I wonder if they're ever going to," remarked Garth,

editor of the *Cot's Crier*, as he sat chewing his fish and chips at Mulchin's.

In response, a murmur of fearful, gloomy voices emanated from the small crowd of locals gathered round Garth's table.

"I don't mean we haven't a decent constabulary with us," Garth continued after swishing his beer around in his mouth. "But the facts are the way they are. Either the man's very ingenious and has left the area entirely, or he's quite incapable and has got himself drowned in the sea."

"Like as not, George Abernathy'd be hopin' for the latter," remarked the butcher.

"Ah, yes, the poor chap," Garth assented. "Very broken up, he is. Twenty-five years of marriage, he told me. She wasn't a kind woman to many folk, but I've a feeling she was different with her man."

"Indeedy," said Barney Mulchin, who was leaning his forearms on the back of the butcher's chair. "Abernathy will need friends about him these days, even if he hasn't tried to make any before. And I think one or two of us who's been standing off ought to start being kind to the man. What do you say, Fraser?"

Clint Fraser was tucked away by himself in a nearby booth. At the mention of his name, he looked up from his drink.

"Eh?" he grunted.

"I said don't you think you ought to do something about Abernathy?" Barney repeated. "You haven't said anything for weeks, but I know you've still been unduly suspicious and unfriendly towards the man. What do you think now, after what's happened this week?"

The old gossip, uncommonly subdued and melancholy, sluggishly arose and fished some change out of his pocket.

"I think," he said, "I should have done somethin' about Abernathy a long time ago."

Then the man clapped the money down upon the table and shambled out of the pub.

⤳⤵

Eva was in her father's bedroom, staring out the window at the rain beating against the glass and weighing down the flowers in the garden. She didn't know what she was doing there or what she was looking for. Perhaps she almost expected to see her father returning the way he had gone nearly three days ago. But there was nothing outside but the rain, the soggy grass, and the dark troop of clouds marching in the gray distance.

"How do you think she's taking it?" someone said.

Eva turned and realized her uncle was standing in the hallway outside her father's closed bedroom door.

"I don't think she is," came her aunt's voice.

"What do you mean?"

"I don't think she's letting herself believe it."

"I'd have a hard time believing it, too, if I was her," Euston indicated. "Actually, I still can't believe it. He wasn't capable of doing anything like that on purpose. It had to be an accident."

"But it still happened, Mort," said Agnes. "The result will be the same. It doesn't matter how it happened."

"I think it does to Eva. I think she's trying to believe it was an accident."

"She's also trying to believe God will bring him back safely," Agnes retorted, her tone turning bitter. "I heard her praying that as I passed by her room last night. The poor child!"

"What's wrong with the kid praying, if it makes her feel better?"

"It's wrong because it's a lie," Agnes returned sharply. "It's an imaginary friend she talks to. And I don't care if one grows out of it in time, but Ulysses never did. He kept up with the prayers

190

and catechisms and Bibles right into adulthood and still went on with the delusion after his wife died. He didn't want to accept the truth. Even when I told him that a God who ignored Ulysses' prayers and good deeds and just let Hazel die either didn't exist or didn't care, he still wouldn't accept it. It wasn't until after the funeral that he admitted he felt the same way sometimes. But even so, he didn't abandon his fantasies. I don't think he ever did.

"Well, I'm not going to let Eva grow up believing in fairy tales, Mort. I'd be some guardian if I did. Ulysses' God didn't do *him* any good, now did He? He goes out to do the right thing, and look what comes of it. No well-done's, no rewards, nothing but a small pension and a mind left in fragments. And now he's likely at the bottom of the sea. No, Mort, it's not harmless to let Eva go about trying to believe in the same rubbish. We can't let that happen to her."

In a moment, the sound of her aunt's and uncle's footsteps faded down the hall, leaving the girl alone again.

Eva felt like something was squeezing her throat shut. She looked up into the weeping sky, but she could think of nothing to say. If Agnes was right that Eva had lost both her father and her God, what words could there be left to say?

Chapter 20

"'Nother five minutes," Euston mumbled. "It can't last much longer."

"I can't either," rasped the young man standing beside him. "It's so, so cold."

"I know, Short," Euston replied, "but the commandant's out tonight. It won't be so long this time. You know he never stays out in the cold."

"Silence!" a guard shouted, waving his rifle threateningly. "No talking in the Standing Line!"

Euston shut his chapped lips and glared in the guard's direction.

"Face forvard!" another German yelled.

Euston turned his head and looked at the rows of pitiful, starving men in front of him. Any man could drop in seconds. It was so cold that it was only a matter of time before someone did.

Wearily, the corporal closed his eyes and tried to bring up a few murky memories of life before Das Grab. They did not come easily these days. Just thinking no longer came easily.

Thud!

Corporal Euston's eyes snapped open, and he looked round as much as he could without moving his head. A soldier had fallen. He could not see who it was.

"*Eins! Zwei! Drei! Vier!*"

They were starting that heaven-forsaken count.

Get up, get up! Euston thought, closing his eyes again. He could hear Short whimpering and sniffling next to him.

"*Acht, neun, zehn!*"

He just had to see who it was. Betting the guards were preoccupied, he turned his head and scanned the men around him. Seeing that no one in front had fallen, he craned his neck to look behind him.

It was one of Short's companions.

"No, no, no," he heard Short murmur.

"Don't look," Euston urged.

"Forvard!" a soldier shrieked, stomping over and striking Euston in the face.

His head reeling, Euston once again stared ahead.

"*Zwanzig!*" the counter shrieked. "Time is up!"

"No!" Short howled, bolting for the fallen soldier.

In that second, Euston and several other men broke formation. Then there was chaos.

"Shoot!" someone screamed. "Fire, fire!"

"No!" Euston shouted, sitting up. "No, stop!"

"Morton!" Agnes gasped, grabbing his arm as he struggled to get out of bed. "Morton, calm down!"

"I'm sorry, I'm sorry," Euston moaned, leaning back and covering his face with his hands.

"Another dream?" Agnes asked.

"Another nightmare," he corrected, turning over in bed. "I'm okay now."

"Sure?"

"Yeah, go to sleep."

In a few minutes both Euston and his wife were asleep again.

But then it was freezing outside.

And his throat ached.

And his muscles screamed.

And he was so, so hungry.

A tall man garbed in black was standing before the eight remaining men in Euston's barracks.

"I am here for a special reason," the man declared in that cold, disgustingly delighted voice of his. "Normally the sergeant of the guard vould see to such a matter, but I have some cause to be interested this time."

He had been pacing back and forth with his gloved hands clasped behind him. Now he paused, adjusted his spectacles, and turned those bright, hawk-like eyes and that white, high-boned face upon the prisoners.

"It is not often somevon steals a pistol from a guard," he revealed with a smile.

Euston glanced at the other men, but they were all looking at one another with the same shock and dread on their faces.

"Gave the man a concussion," chuckled the German. "Very spirited. Very daring, ya?"

Euston swallowed hard and clasped his shivering hands at his sides.

"Now," the officer continued, pacing once again, "I like spirit, so I vill be fair. If the man responsible vill step forvard, I vill not kill all of you. You have ten seconds."

Fearfully, Euston considered the prisoners around him, wondering which one of them had stolen the firearm. He couldn't believe anyone would be so foolhardy.

The seconds ticked by, but no one moved to confess. An animal panic was etched in the faces of every Allied soldier. Surely no one had done it.

"Commandant, sir," spoke Lieutenant Ryder, one of the last Allied officers left, "there must be some mistake."

"There is none," the commandant replied. "Five seconds."

"But sir—"

"Three. Two," droned the commandant. "Very vell, everyvone—"

"I did it," someone said faintly.

All eyes turned to see Sergeant Starbuck taking a slow step forward. His body was bent and wasted, his face still bruised and swollen from the day before. Even so, he stood staring resolutely into the commandant's pitiless face.

The commandant's mouth curled into a sneer.

"Very vell," the officer returned coolly. "Take him."

At once, two guards seized Ulysses and started to drag him stumbling away.

But Euston knew the sergeant was lying. He also knew the man could not survive what they were about to do to him.

"No, wait!" Euston cried. "I did it!"

The guards stopped and looked questioningly at the commandant.

"Ah, the brave American," the commandant snickered, strolling over to him. "Confessing at last, are ve?"

"I did it," Euston bobbed his head. "You can let him go, 'cause it was me."

"Really? Vere is the veapon?"

"I panicked and threw it away."

The commandant leaned down to within inches of the corporal's face.

"Ve both know you're lying," he whispered. "Guards, take the sergeant to my special room. I shall be there soon."

"But he didn't do it!" Euston argued passionately. "He didn't! He's lying! Sergeant, tell them it was me!"

"The man who did this," the commandant said, calmly taking off his glasses and rubbing streaks of melting snow from the lenses, "he vould not have confessed."

He turned to follow the guards.

"What are you doing?" Euston cried. "You're going to punish the wrong man!"

The commandant paused and looked over his shoulder.

"I know," he said, and walked away.

Euston watched the man with horror. Then slowly he grasped what the commandant had told him. And he knew just who was responsible for this, the man who really stole the pistol, the man who was now standing passively by letting someone else take the punishment for him again.

"Selkirk!" he shouted.

"Darling, what's wrong?"

Euston opened his eyes. He was back in bed.

"Are you sure you're all right?" Agnes pressed. "I could get you something for sleep."

"No, I'm fine," said Euston, getting up and fumbling for his robe.

"Where are you going?"

"Just getting some fresh air."

"I'll come with you."

"No, baby, it's okay," Euston said with a wave of his hand. "Go on back to sleep."

Morton Euston was headed for the back door, but he never made it that far. As soon as he reached the kitchen, he fell into a chair by the table and dropped his head into his hands. And there in the stillness and the dark of that room, Corporal Euston sat alone—and cried.

If it weren't a long hour's bicycle ride to the village, and if the cliffs upon which its rolling green pastures rested weren't too tall to allow access to the shore below, it would have been absolutely perfect. But, while the family sometimes regretted the distance to town or the beach, they could all still agree that the Butterfield farm was a little country-bred paradise.

Even so, keeping up the paradise was a constant strain upon Jeremiah Butterfield, Mandy's father. He had lost part of his left arm during the war, rendering him reliant on the aid of his sons Ira and Desmond and the farm's one hired hand Ferguson. Jeremiah was an independent man and deeply hated being helpless for any reason. Sometimes he hated it worse than others.

"Maggie!" he bellowed, kicking the back door shut.

His wife, accustomed to these sudden eruptions, went on dicing carrots and humming to herself without a reply to her spouse.

"Where is Desmond?" Jeremiah fumed, stomping into the kitchen.

"Did you wipe your feet?"

"Yes. Where is he?"

"Down at the garage," his wife responded.

"I told him I needed him today!"

"Sit down, dear," Maggie said, pushing his broad figure into a chair. "Now remember he has to work today. You said you understood that."

"Well," her husband grumbled, "never was a worse day for him to be gone. I found the south gate open. No doubt it was left that way by some fool from the Rambler's Association, and at least six sheep are missin' because of him. Wolf is sick, and he's my best dog for findin' them. I sent Ferguson lookin', but he'll need help."

"What about Daisy?" Maggie offered. "She's good at that sort of thing, isn't she?"

"Cor, I could kill that dog!" Mr. Butterfield exclaimed, slamming his one calloused fist upon the starchy tablecloth. "I can't keep her at home this week. Wanderin' off to who knows where any time she pleases! I hate tyin' her up durin' the day, but that's just what I had to do this mornin'."

"She's still a pup, Jerry. She'll learn eventually."

"And did you hear her last night? Howlin' to wake the dead! I went out and told her off, but she started it up again as soon as I was gone. I finally let her go just to get her away, but you could still hear her yowlin' off in the fields. It comes of you and Mandy spoilin' the dog like it was a pet."

"Why does she howl, I wonder?" said Maggie. "She hasn't done it before, you know."

"I don't know," Jeremiah replied, throwing his hand into the air.

"My mother used to say a dog howls that way when someone is going to die," mused the farmer's wife.

"She probably wants to come in the house. I told you not to let Mandy bring her in."

"Of course, it's really just a superstition," Maggie admitted. "But I remember my old retriever howled for days before my grandfather died. He never howled again after that. Maybe dogs sense that sort of thing. Do you think so, Jerry?"

"There she goes again!" her husband trumpeted, jumping up. "Hear her in the barn! By George, I'd rather her be wanderin' the countryside than puttin' the sheep on edge with that wailin'. I'm turnin' her loose again. If she wants to come back, then she will."

Mr. Butterfield thundered off like an angry god leaving Olympus, while his wife stood with her head cocked to one side, listening to the eerie whining and caterwauling coming from the barn.

"Doesn't make sense," she said at length, shaking her head and returning to her vegetables. "And superstition or no, it makes me uneasy."

"I'll knock again," said Major Arnold, drumming his fist upon the door a few more times, "just to be safe."

"He's not there," Clint Fraser informed him. "You can jest go right in."

"I'll do no such thing," Arnold returned. "There are procedures we follow in the British Army, and no one would be safe if we didn't."

"I was at the Battle o' the Somme durin' the Great War," Fraser said. "We didn't always have time to follow procedures."

Arnold tried to peer through one of the nearby windows until he finally sighed in disgust.

"Someone will have my head for this," he grumbled. "From all Holt tells me, I was mad to believe your story in the first place. And I don't believe it, sir. But we investigate things like this, and sometimes we do it whether we believe in them or not."

"One o' the back windows has a broken lock," Fraser suggested. "D'you want to get in and see it or not?"

"If it's really true, why didn't you report it at once?" the major asked, ignoring the man's suggestion.

"I'm shamed to say it, sir," Fraser said, shaking his head, "but when you spend your life makin' every mole's hill a mountain for the benefit o' your mates, you eventually can't tell the difference between the two anymore. I'm afeared it took somebody dyin' for me to see the difference."

The major looked at the old sailor for a moment.

"You really believe this, don't you?" he said.

"I believe what I see."

"So do I. Which window is it?"

A few minutes and a couple tight squeezes later, Major Arnold and Clint Fraser were standing in the Abernathy's bedroom. Aside from a light layer of dust and a general stuffiness about the place, the room and the rest of the house looked as though they belonged to a perfectly normal Scottish couple. A quick examination revealed that George Abernathy was not there.

"Where is it, then?" Arnold hissed, keeping his voice down despite the house's vacancy.

Fraser led the officer back to the bedroom and pointed to the closet.

"Surely they wouldn't keep anything secret in there," Arnold scoffed. "That's the first place anyone would look."

"I don't think they expected anyone to be lookin'," Clint reasoned.

Arnold strode over, and, after declaring again that someone would have his head, he turned the knob and swung the door back.

"Impossible," he murmured.

"D'you believe me now?"

Arnold nodded but said nothing. For there, hanging from the back of the closet door and staring back at the two men with its bold, crimson visage, was the death flag of the Nazi Third Reich.

Chapter 21

Ulysses Starbuck was dead. No one announced it, but it was so all the same. Ten days after Sally Abernathy was murdered, Inspector Downes called off the search. A British Army psychiatrist and Dr. McCabe both agreed that Ulysses' poor mental functioning brought the chances of him surviving that long alone in the elements to almost nothing. The man had killed a woman and then got his deserts by dying himself. His body had been swept out to sea. For the village, that was the end of it.

But somehow it didn't feel right to Halsted Holt. Although he was a man with a thick head and a bulldog determination to be correct at the first, he just couldn't put something out of his mind this time.

When he thought about it, there really was a plentiful amount of evidence. Or rather, there seemed to be evidence in the wrong places. Holt remembered the night they mistook blood on Eva Starbuck for Roger Wyatt's, and he wondered— just wondered, mind—if they hadn't made the same mistake again.

Of course, in the beginning there had been no reason to

think Ulysses Starbuck was bleeding the day he killed Sally Abernathy, but perhaps he had been. And if he had, then why?

∽◦

"He should have died in Germany."

"Wha'?" Euston asked, pausing with his toothbrush in his mouth.

"Ulysses," Agnes said.

"Why do you say that?" Euston replied, looking up from the washbasin in their bedroom.

"Because," Agnes sighed, "he would have suffered less. We would have suffered less. He would have died and been honored as a good soldier who did he duty."

"But he was a good soldier," Euston pointed out. "I never knew a better one."

"I know. But no one will remember him for that. In the end, not even Eva will. He'll be remembered as that madman who murdered a nurse. That's all."

"Agnes, you don't know what you're saying."

"Oh, but I do, Mort," his wife contended, her eyes flashing darkly. "Do you know what they're saying in the village? They're polite, of course, and not speaking it to our faces, but I've heard more than they think. 'Deserved no less. Lucky we are that killer's gone. God's given him his dues at last.' That's what they're saying, Mort. It turns my stomach that such people sit comfortably at home and speak those foul things with their tea in hand, listening to the BBC on the radio and not even realizing that men like Ulysses lost their lives so they could say and do what they please."

"We don't know he's dead, Agnes," said Morton. "That's what that detective Downes thinks, but he can't prove it yet. Ulysses survived six months after he was abandoned in Germany. I know he had more of his mental—eh—skills then, but my point is he knew how to survive. Downes could easily wrong."

"Oh, I hope he's right," his wife returned passionately.

"Agnes!"

"Have you been listening at all?" she asked. "If he were alive, it would still be the same. Only they'd put him away to die in some cold institution where men are treated like animals. Of course I want him to be dead! It's better that way! You would feel the same as I do if you'd watched helplessly as the one person you loved more than anything wasted away and died raving while doctors stood by and observed him like a specimen under a microscope!"

Eva's aunt stopped and dug her nails into her palms.

"Why did he do this to us, Mort?" she continued brokenly. "Why did he have to kill her? All the time he was with us, I never asked what was wrong with him. I just loved him and did what I could for him. But I didn't understand. The man who came back from the war wasn't my brother. He wasn't anything like my brother!"

Euston set his toothbrush down and leaned back against the washstand.

"Agnes," he said after a deep breath, "you've never asked me what happened to your brother in Das Grab. I don't think you want to know everything that happened. I don't know if I could tell you. But I have to tell you something, so you can understand."

Agnes sat down on the edge of the bed and looked up at her husband.

"It was always awful," Euston began. "But a couple months before the sergeant escaped, it got even worse for him. One night, the commandant got him, and we didn't see him for two days. When they brought him back, I took one look at him and knew that something in the sergeant was gone. I didn't know what it was at first, but I think I know now. They got his hope, Agnes. They got the only thing that had kept his mind and soul together. And before he even made it home, the loss of that hope must have killed him."

Agnes cleared her throat and blinked rapidly.

"Baby," Euston said, "all this beauty that your brother's had around him since he came back—his family, his home—he's only seen that by accident sometimes. He hasn't been here with you and Eva where things are better. Those moments when I feel like I'm back in the camp aren't moments for him. That's where he lives. Your brother isn't lost out there in the countryside: he still hasn't made it out of Das Grab."

Terrence Farrier was so nervous. Here he was, striding down the beach with Mandy Butterfield's arm through his. He was not even sure how it happened. He didn't known Mandy felt anything special for him until last month after he rescued her Sunday hat from falling into a puddle. As the vicar's son and a well-mannered young gentleman, he didn't think much of the act. But Mandy did.

All through that month, she wore him down with her persuasive nature, determination, and irresistibly huge eyes, until they were going as "steady" as a thirteen- and fourteen-year-old can.

The poor fellow hadn't the foggiest idea of what to do about it. To say no to such a nice girl felt like a sin. So, every week they went for a stroll and then tea at a café that charged rather more than Terrence could afford. And each week, all he could think about was how many hedges he had trimmed for that money, and how tightly she was squeezing his arm, and how very badly he was sweating, and how nice it would be if only Christ would hurry up and come back for God's children about then (or at least before the next teatime).

"Ready to turn round?" Terrence asked with a crackling voice.

"What, right now?" Mandy questioned. "Why, Terry, we've only been walking ten minutes!"

It was more like half an hour to Terrence, but he couldn't be certain.

"Let's go a bit further, until we get to the taller cliffs near the farm," Mandy suggested, squeezing his small bicep even tighter.

Hopefully, Terrence looked ahead, but his countenance fell when he saw what a long way it was before the cliffs grew taller.

It really was not so long a journey. Within fifteen minutes, the two children were striding under the looming gray giants that guard the southern spurs of Great Britain. If they gazed upward and ahead, they could just descry cottony puffs of sheep grazing the green grass atop the cliffs.

"Isn't it lovely?" Mandy cooed, snuggling into the bony arm of her uneasy sweetheart.

"Yes, ready to turn round now?"

"Hmm, let's go a little further, to that big drift log up there," Mandy suggested, pointing. "Then we can go back."

To Terrence, elated by the idea of turning back, another hundred yards was a few steps. So on they walked, with Mandy happily lost in memories of romance novels and Terrence keeping his gaze firmly on that drift log of salvation.

But as they strolled, a curious thing happened before Terrence's eyes. That log began changing shape. And the closer they got, the less like a log that log became. In fact, it started to look like something very familiar.

Terrence pulled up sharp and short, like a horse that has spotted an unknown dog in the road.

"What's the matter?" asked Mandy.

The boy was lifting his hand to point, but he changed his mind.

"Mandy," he said, "why don't you stand here a moment? Just stop right here, you understand, and don't follow me."

"What are you talking about, Terry?"

"Maybe nothing," replied the boy, "but there might be something dangerous ahead, and I think I should look at it first."

"A jellyfish?"

"If you like. Stay here, please."

Exuberant about the idea of Terrence protecting her from something, Mandy consented to his wish without another question and stood proudly watching him start off down the beach.

Terrence walked swiftly. Soon he was near enough to know without a doubt that what Mandy had mistaken for a drift log was something else entirely. Five feet from the object, the boy stopped abruptly. Then he turned and raced back to Mandy as fast as he could.

"Come on!" he shouted, catching her arm and dragging her along with him.

"Terry, what's wrong?" Mandy cried.

"We've got to find the chief constable!"

"But what *was* it?"

"A body," Terrence panted. "A dead body!"

⌒○

Major Arnold sat behind a desk in the second-best bedroom of Mrs. Gentry's Boarding House in Cot's Haven. Mrs. Gentry might not have approved of it, but he had spent the past hour filling that tidy, flower-papered room with cigarette smoke. Before him was a leather journal, worn at the edges and stained with time and use. He had been staring at the cover for some time.

Finally, he took a deep breath and opened the book. With brisk determination, he thumbed many pages penned in a neat, careful hand. Near the end of the journal, Arnold stopped thumbing. With a trembling finger, he traced over the heading at the top of a page:

23 March 1945: Execution of Lt. Philip Ryder

At once, he stood up, snatched the volume, and hurled it against the wall with a bang.

Thump, thump!

"What!" Arnold shouted at the door.

"Major, there's someone on the telephone asking for you," the landlady announced from the hall.

"Thank you, Mrs. Gentry," said the major, drawing a hand across his distressed countenance.

"Is everything all right, Major?"

"Yes, thank you," Arnold replied, leaning forward heavily against the desk. "Everything is fine."

⌒◦

In forty-five minutes, Constable Holt was on the beach, along with the doctor, Major Arnold, and Terrence Farrier.

"It's George Abernathy, you know," the policeman revealed, pushing the man's face into better view with his foot. "Even with all the damage, you can still see it. How long's he been dead, doctor?"

"Two days at least," McCabe determined, standing up. "Of course, the police surgeon will know more later, but it's obvious to me he died of the fall."

"Fall?" Terrence asked nervously.

"From the cliff. Oh, Terrence, you can go home now. You don't seem keen on this business."

The boy thanked the doctor and scurried away from the dreadful scene.

"Must'a been quite a trip down," Holt grunted grimly. "See the look on the man's face!"

"Yes, his face," Arnold mumbled, lighting a cigarette. "Constable, I'd like someone to identify this man as soon as possible, while he's still halfway recognizable."

"Why do you want to do a thing like that?" Holt returned. "I know him by sight. It's George Abernathy, all right."

"I'm sure it is," the major snapped. "But I said *someone*, not you. You can see it's Abernathy. I don't want your opinion."

Holt scratched his salt-and-pepper scalp and scowled.

"I have a feeling the Army has some special interest in this," McCabe said, glancing at Arnold, "else the major wouldn't have stayed on after the search was called off. I would do as the man asks, Halsted."

"I was planning to," the constable grumbled.

"Major, you might be interested to hear that this man didn't just happen to trip and fall off the cliff," the doctor added.

"Oh?" Holt interjected. "How do you know?"

"His jacket's ripped here," said the doctor, poking at the spot with a stick. "A great deal of force went into that, for it was a quality jacket and immaculately cared for. Someone tore it. And four of his fingernails are broken. Then there's some hair missing from his head. I also bring to your attention the expression on the man's face: he was rather more angry than surprised, if you ask me. By itself it means little, for men have died alone with such a face. However, when considered with everything else—"

"Are you telling me *he* was murdered, too?" Holt exclaimed.

"You have yet to convince me his wife was," McCabe returned. "A man can be killed without being murdered. All I am telling you is that you won't get far thinking Abernathy was just taking a pleasant walk and happened to trip on a stone and tumble to his death. There was someone else involved when he met his end."

"I agree with you, doctor," the major commented.

"Just what I thought," said Holt. "Now I don't know what you want him for, Major, but you shall have this man on a slab and ready to be identified by your *someone* in short order. In the meantime, I've got a thing or two to investigate myself."

Eva would not leave the house. She refused to eat anything. She did not want to see anyone. She didn't talk, or cry. She simply sat in her room, scratched her dirty head, and stared thoughtlessly out the window. She had been this way for three days, ever since the police abandoned the search for her father.

Agnes was worried. Though she tried talking to Eva, preparing her favorite meals, and suggesting a holiday, none of that helped. When Grace Tankard stopped by to offer the Starbucks her support and prayers, Eva wouldn't even emerge from her room to see her old friend. At last, Agnes telephoned the doctor for help, but McCabe said a doctor wasn't what Eva needed. Agnes did not know what to do.

Someone else did.

Late in the afternoon on Eva's third day alone, someone knocked on her bedroom door.

"Go away, please," she said.

She expected to be left by herself again, for her aunt had always gone away at those words; but this time the person knocked again.

"I said please go away."

"I won't," said the knocker. "Let me in."

With a moan, Eva tucked her hair behind her ears.

"Fine," she replied.

Promptly the door opened, and in stepped Harold York. Closing the door behind him, he plopped onto Eva's desk chair, crossed his ankle over his knee, and looked at her.

Eva did not mean to, but just then she gave him a very oily glare.

"Hungry?" Harold queried.

"No."

"Mind if I?"

As she waved her hand in assent, Harold produced a bag of lemon drops from his pocket and popped two into his mouth.

"Did you come here to eat candy?" Eva asked.

The boy shook his head.

"Well, why then?"

Harold just shrugged; his mouth was too full to speak. Heaving a sigh, Eva turned back to the window and stared through it at the newly empty house across the street. She could hear Harold crunching the hard candy and swallowing loudly.

"I don't want to talk," Eva said at length.

"Neither do I," Harold agreed.

"It's been one bad thing after another these past nine months. I feel like I've come to the end of an awful story, and there's nothing left to it."

Eva glanced at Harold. He was staring back at her, leaning forward with his chin cupped in his palm.

"You can leave anytime, you know," said the girl.

"I know."

"But you won't, will you?"

"Probably not. Unless you want me to go."

"Well, I do."

"No, you don't."

"I do!"

"Want a lemon drop?"

"No!" Eva shouted.

There was a pause, and Eva twisted uncomfortably.

"I'm sorry," she muttered. "I don't really want you to go, Harold."

"I know."

"I don't know how you stand me."

"Me neither," Harold replied with a smirk.

"No, but I really mean it, Harold," the girl insisted. "When Roger was around, I was so beastly and unfair to you. I knew inside that I really didn't love him, but I didn't want to think about it. I knew he wasn't what I wanted. When I thought about it, I realized I don't want anyone that way right now."

"Me neither," the boy replied. "I'm just your friend, Eva. I always have been. I haven't pretended to be anything else. I wasn't jealous of you and Roger the way you thought. I only wanted to protect you."

Eva smiled, but her face soon clouded over again.

"All I really wanted was my father," she sighed. "And now I shan't ever have him. Harold, it doesn't make sense. Why does God let these things happen? Aunty says a God like that isn't worth believing in, and sometimes I could agree with her. I know it's wrong, Harold, but that's how I feel. Why can't things be like they are in good books, where the story ends with the people living happily ever after?"

"I don't know, Eva," Harold admitted. "I don't understand Him sometimes either. But I don't think He means to be understood. I think He just wants us to believe Him. You know, believe Him when He says all the things He wrote about Himself are true. And really, we don't need to make sense of something to believe it."

"But it makes it awfully hard."

"I know, and I'm sure He does, too."

"Why did you come, Harold?" Eva asked suddenly.

"Just to eat candy," returned the boy. "I hate eating alone. Want one?"

"Well," Eva mused, looking at the proffered bag, "I suppose so."

❦❧

"But I've never even seen George Abernathy!" Euston protested, following the major down a white-tiled hallway in the county morgue. "I work in Eastbourne, Major; I haven't met half the people in Cot's Haven."

"Perfect," said Arnold.

"But how do you expect me to identify a man I don't know?"

"I don't expect you to do that. Here we are, through this door."

Flabbergasted, Euston stepped into a frigid room whose walls were lined with stacks of numbered metal doors. At the officer's direction, an attendant opened one of these and rolled out a shrouded corpse.

"Just tell me what you think," Arnold instructed.

Shaking his head, Euston walked over and peered under the sheet.

Almost at once his face blanched as white as the tiled floor beneath him.

"Oh, no," he breathed, taking a step back and looking with horror at the major.

"I thought so," said Arnold.

"This—*this* is her husband?" Euston asked, pointing at the dead man. "This?"

"I'm afraid so."

"Oh, no!" the engineer repeated, weakly grabbing a chair. "And we let her take care of the sergeant day after day! I just can't believe it! They must have planned it!"

"Whether they did or not," replied the officer, "the fact remains. For months, your little village has been harboring one of the men most wanted during the Nuremberg trials—the commandant of Das Grab."

Chapter 22

"He was crazy, you know," said Euston. "I can't tell you how relieved I am that he's dead."

The two soldiers had left the morgue and were now ensconced in a corner booth at a nearby pub. The major leaned back against the cushioned seat and folded his arms across his chest.

"Between you and me," he replied, "I regret his death, because I wish I had done the deed myself. Hundreds of good men died by his villainy; he deserved far worse than what he got."

"You know, he called himself a collector," Euston shook his head, holding up his three-fingered right hand. "He took these for every escape attempt. He took our rations if a man was too slow to roll call. He took what blankets and shoes we had if our work wasn't done fast enough. He took men's lives and men's sanity every single day, and he enjoyed every minute of it."

Euston paused and rubbed his temples.

"Sometimes I think I'm there again," he muttered. "I'll have a dream, or someone will say something. Major, I heard a guy counting the other day, and it brought everything back. That camp is always with me, in some dark place in my mind. And no matter what I do, I can't make it go away."

"I'm afraid I must ask you to visit that place again," answered the major. "We need answers, and there is no other way to get at them."

"Sure, I understand."

"Since the day Das Grab was raided and we discovered the commandant had escaped us, the British Army searched for this man," the officer said. "All our efforts turned up nothing. If Clint Fraser hadn't come to me, I would never have looked in Abernathy's closet and found the commandant's journals recording his private executions. No one would have known George Abernathy was the name the commandant was hiding behind. He would have been safe."

"Told you he was insane."

"But to take up residence in Cot's Haven, the home of one of the only survivors of the camp, could not have been an accident, though it was an incredible risk," the major continued. "When he came to the village, he had no guarantee of Starbuck's feeble state of mind. He chanced ruin and ultimately execution if Starbuck identified him. Why go to Cot's Haven at all? There are ten thousand places for such a man to hide and remain unnoticed for the rest of his life. Can you guess why the commandant would take that chance just to live near Ulysses Starbuck?"

"That's easy," Euston smiled wryly, "He was always obsessed with the sergeant. That German fed on hope and willpower like some sort of parasite. He could wring it out of you as easy as water from a sponge. But not the sergeant. No, he couldn't get to the sergeant. And that made him so angry that he hauled Ulysses into his 'special room' almost every day to deal him the worst kinds of punishments. I think he sensed that Ulysses was the only man in that camp that he really couldn't break, at least not without a long fight. And he hated things he couldn't break.

"If you want to know what I think, it's this: I think he came to Cot's Haven to finish the job he started in Das Grab. I think he came to break the sergeant and finally take his hope. He must not have realized that he already did."

⌒⊙

"You let her go?" Mandy gasped the next morning at breakfast, her expressive mouth flinging open.

"Yes, I did," her father replied.

"But why?" the girl whined, tears forming in her eyes.

"Because she was puttin' the sheep on edge with her howlin'. Now she howled all Saturday night and all yesterday, and neither the sheep nor I could take it any longer. She yammered for a week straight last time, and I wasn't about to wait around for her to stop this time. I know she's your dog, but I told you when I gave her to you that she's part of the farm first. She'll come back when she's hungry, so button your mouth back up and stop waterin' your egg."

Mandy was going to say something, but she decided against it. She had learned years ago that her father was immune to her very best displays of melodrama. Although he cared very much if something truly important happened, he refused to let her mope about insignificant rubbish. Daisy being set loose classified as insignificant rubbish.

"May I go look for Daisy, at least?" she asked after a bite of her egg.

"Sure. Just don't bring her back on a lead, and don't wander off the farm," said her father.

"And stay away from the cliffs," Mrs. Butterfield instructed. "Especially after that poor Mr. Abernathy's accident, I don't want you near them."

So, straight after breakfast Mandy put on her rainboots and an old skirt and started off through the fields, calling for her dog.

Meanwhile, her father and her brother Ira headed for the barn to gather tools for a gate they were repairing in the south field.

"Well, hallo, Butterfield!" boomed Chief Constable Holt, shooting from behind the barndoor like an overweight jack-in-the-box.

"What the devil are you doin' in there?" Jeremiah demanded.

"Checking up on a case, you know," came the reply.

"No, I don't know. What's it about?"

"I'm afraid I can't say," Holt stated mysteriously, "but I would like to ask you and your family a few questions."

"Make 'em short, then. We have things to do."

"Just one or two, now. Hallo, Ira!"

"Chief Constable," Ira greeted, touching his hat. "Has it got to do with Mr. Abernathy?"

"Well, just a bit. Routine, you know. Did anyone happen to see him walking in this area a few days ago?"

The farmers shook their heads.

"Seen anyone else?"

"No."

"Anything unusual happen lately?"

"Nothin'," said Jeremiah.

"Well, yes," Ira replied.

"What, then?" his father questioned, annoyed by the further delay. "I haven't noticed anythin'."

"It's not much," Ira acknowledged with a shrug, "but it's odd. One of the dogs has been howlin'."

"Oh, has it?" Holt said, raising his brows and producing a pad and pen. "How long has it been howling?"

"Couple days this time. But she cried for a week until Mr. Abernathy died, and then she just stopped. I never heard a dog howl like that before, sir. It sounded awful."

"She howls when she's tied up," Jeremiah inserted irritably.

"If she wanders, I put her in the barn, and she doesn't like it. That's why she howls."

"Well, yes. But she keeps howlin' when she's loose," Ira noted. "Seems odd to me, that's all."

"Seems unusual to me, too," Holt agreed, scribbling vigorously in his notebook.

"Good for you," Jeremiah grunted. "Now, if you don't mind, while you go off and waste your time on dogs and old superstitions, we'll go and start on our gate."

"Well, I don't suppose it's any harm. Go right ahead."

Holt snapped his notebook shut with great authority. He was about to walk away when he stopped and cocked his head.

"Did you hear that?" he asked.

"It came from over there!" Ira exclaimed, motioning toward the cliffs.

"There it is again!" Holt announced.

"Cor, it's Mandy that's screamin'!" Jeremiah shouted. "Come on, lads!"

The three men took off like a small stampede of buffalo. Following the noise, they eventually spotted Mandy scrambling over a stone wall ahead of them. She was shrieking and waving her arms with all the passion of a small body hit with an uncontrollable surge of adrenaline.

"Mandy!" her father bellowed, jogging over and catching her just as she sprang from the wall. "What the devil is it?"

"Father!" she squealed, choking him with her grip. "Make it go away!"

"Make what go away?"

"Make them stop! I don't want to see them anymore!" she yelped. "Not another one of them, please! I didn't want to see Mr. Aber—Aber—I didn't want to see him dead, Father! But now it's Mr. Starbuck, and I just can't bear it! It's so awful!"

Her father looked ill.

"Mandy girl, where is he?" he questioned.

But as he spoke, the high-pitched, mournful wails of a dog echoed across the fields.

"My money's on your dog!" Holt proclaimed and trotted off following the noise.

"Take your sister home, Ira," Jeremiah ordered, bending down and peeling his daughter off his neck. "Daisy's in the south field. Come as soon as you can."

When Jeremiah reached the south field, he found Holt standing near the cliff. Several feet away from him sat Daisy. Her ears were back, and a low, rumbling growl issued from her throat.

"Daisy, heel!" the farmer commanded as he approached.

Seeing her master, the young border collie let out a whine and pattered obediently to his side. As the dog moved away, the two men could see what she had been guarding: huddled beside a large stone a few feet from the cliff was the body of Ulysses Starbuck.

Constable Holt stepped over to it and shook his head.

"Here's our missing man at last," he sighed. "We should've kept looking."

"Isn't this the place where George Abernathy went over?" asked the farmer. "That means two men died here. It's a grim place, isn't it?"

"Well," said Holt, picking up one of Ulysses' wrists and feeling for a pulse, "this one's not quite dead."

"Not quite dead" was about all that could be said for Eva's father. He had been missing fourteen days, and he looked it. Smeared with mud and debris from the recent rains, bruised and scraped from head to toe, he looked like something left behind by a hurricane.

"Missing a finger, I see," Holt commented, examining Ulysses' right hand with interest.

"Missin' a few, I'd say," said the farmer.

"Yes, but this one's recent. It's not healed up like the others. Tells me a lot, it does."

At the sound of voices, Ulysses stirred, opened one eye, and glanced listlessly up at the constable.

"I don't know what you're made of," Holt said, lightly thumping the man on the shoulder, "but it's something built to last. Butterfield, when your boy gets here, we'll take him back and call the doctor, eh?"

"Why?"

"Why what?"

"Well," said the farmer, "isn't he the fellow who murdered the Abernathy woman?"

"*Killed*," the constable corrected. "There's a difference, you know. I daresay we'll all be learning a lesson from this, Butterfield. I'm afraid we've been too sure of things. I don't doubt we'll be finding the truth out shortly."

"And what do you think the truth is?"

"That Starbuck isn't a savage murderer," Holt replied. "I'd say that if anyone in Cot's Haven had been him, they'd have done what he did, too. Ah, here's Ira," he declared a moment later. "Now, hoist him gently, men. It's a long way back to the house."

Chapter 23

"Hallo, Selkirk," Arnold said, stepping into the cell.

With a face devoid of hope, the young man looked up at the officer.

"I'm glad you came," he said.

"They told me you confessed."

"Yes, I did, sir."

"Why did you ask to see me?"

"Because, Major," Selkirk replied, "I wanted you to hear from me that I didn't hate Marvin Short, and I didn't hate the sergeant. I didn't steal Marvin's tags, leave the sergeant to die, or blame Marvin's death on the sergeant because I hated them. Both of them were nothing but good to me. I just couldn't die. Do you understand? That's why I did it. I was so afraid to die."

"Frankly, I have no interest in the motives for your disgusting behavior," Arnold returned. "What I do want to know is why you bothered to confess that you conspired to murder Marvin Short. I had no proof against you, Selkirk. No one did. As much as it galls me to admit it, you could have walked free."

"I wouldn't have been free," Selkirk said quietly. "I don't know if you can understand, but all through the war I was terrified of

221

dying. I only wanted to live through it, and I didn't care how I did it. But then when the war was over, it was living with myself that really scared me. Every day I'd wake up and wish I had not. Every night I'd lie down and see Marvin, what he looked like just before they took him away; and I'd see the sergeant, lying there dying on that hill while I was off stuffing my face at a farmer's cot; and I'd see all the others, over and over again. And they'd all come up and say, 'Well, was it worth it, Selkirk?'

"I had to confess, Major. I had to make sure I was punished for what I did," the young man explained, wringing his hands. "I couldn't go on with that guilt any longer. I wanted justice to be served."

"Then I suppose we are finished here," replied the major, rapping on the cell door.

"It wasn't worth it, Major," said Selkirk.

"It never is."

That night, Major Arnold closed his files on Starbuck, Short, and Selkirk. The nagging feeling of something being out of place was gone. He had done his duty. The story was over.

Unfortunately, so was another story.

"I'm sorry about Lieutenant Ryder, sir," said Cummings as the major handed him the case files. "I didn't have the pleasure of knowing your nephew, but I understand he was a fine officer."

"He was," Arnold acknowledged. "Did you know, Cummings, it was my idea that he join the British Army? A few years ago, he wanted to be a doctor, but I said a career in the military was what gave a man adventure and fulfillment. Of course, like a good lad he listened to his uncle. Amusing, isn't it?"

"He might have been called to serve his country anyway, sir," the secretary mentioned. "They called them all, from doctors to ditch-diggers."

"Yes, but they called soldiers first. I made him a soldier, and I shall never forget that. Neither shall his mother. He might have been studying to be a doctor; they might have kept him in England. He might not have been tortured to death in Das Grab. I can't forget that, and I won't.

"You know, I was just thinking, Cummings," he added, vigorously grinding the butt of another cigarette into his ashtray, "there must be a reason for it all, mustn't there? I'm talking about my nephew, Sergeant Starbuck, Marvin Short, and the rest of them. There must be a reason for this endless pain over the centuries. It's got to make sense to someone *somewhere* in this universe. If not, then what are we? Why are we here? Why do we bother? Why did my sister's only boy spill his blood for the freedom of a nation that may be dissolved in a hundred years? Why did I spend these months trying to bring justice and truth to a single case in an endless pile of others on this desk? Surely!" he exclaimed fervently. "Surely it can't all be for nothing!"

The secretary stood blinking at his superior officer. He had no idea what to say. He had never seen the major like this.

"I'm afraid I haven't thought much about any of that, sir," he responded at last.

"Well, that's all right, lad," returned the major, instantly regaining his composure. "It's not your fault. I see I've kept you rather late. You may go home now if you like."

"Thank you, sir. I do have some work left, though."

"Leave it until the morning," Arnold replied, saluting the secretary off. "Good night."

After Cummings departed, Major Arnold lit another cigarette and went back to his work. Buried were the words he had spoken moments before, and the emotions that evoked them. He couldn't think about that now. Now, all he could do was keep working.

And while he worked, he could secretly hope that, when the sun came up, somehow it would all look differently.

∽⌒

It was a lovely day. A cool wind herded flocks of clouds across the sky and uncovered the blushing August sun overhead. The white cottages near the cliffs shone like polished pearls, and the grassy turf gleamed with emerald hues; for it had stormed the night before, and the whole world was washed anew.

Down on the pebbled strand there stood a little group of blue and yellow beach chairs facing the water. The Starbucks and Eustons were spending a day by the sea.

It was to be their last day by the sea.

Agnes sat in her bright dress and floppy straw hat, staring out at the waves. But her countenance did not match the mood of her attire or the scene in which she was a part. Her face was drawn with anxiety. Her thin fingers clutched the arms of her chair in a death grip. Inside, she was in turmoil.

"It's going to be okay," her husband said, walking over and squeezing her shoulder reassuringly. "Really, Agnes, I mean it. This won't be like it was with your first husband. Things are better these days, and it's a private mental hospital. He's going to be fine."

Agnes glanced at her brother. He was leaned back in his chair, sleeping dreamlessly by the water.

"He didn't do anything wrong," she said. "Ulysses isn't dangerous, Mort. Just because his mind is damaged and he can't behave like everyone else, they think he will kill again and want him sent away. If he were only himself again, they'd treat him like a hero instead of a leper. He was only defending himself, Mort. He didn't mean to kill her. And who could blame him if he meant to kill *him?*"

"I know, baby," Euston affirmed. "And maybe we can get the right people to see it that way, eventually. I haven't given up, and I know Major Arnold and Holt haven't, either. I think it's pretty good of the magistrate to let us keep him as long as we have. But until he gets better, he needs to go to the hospital."

"*If* he gets better," Agnes muttered under her breath.

"Speaking of the hospital," Euston went on, glancing at his watch, "we need to leave in a half hour."

"I have to finish packing his things."

"I'll help you, then. You just call Eva, and I'll wake him up."

"No, Mort, don't," Agnes objected, putting her hand on his arm. "Give them a little time together. She's not coming with us, anyway. I want her to remember him here at home, out in the sunlight."

Eva had already said goodbye to her father. She had said goodbye over and over, when he left to fight in the war, when he did not come home, when he died, when he vanished, when he died again. She had said goodbye so many times that her heart was weary of it. Inside her there was still grief, but she had cried all the tears that her eyes would allow. She was not calloused. She was not uncaring. She had simply said her farewells and couldn't say them again.

So, while her aunt and uncle grabbed a chair or two and headed back up the cliff path to their cottage, Eva returned to shell-hunting several yards from where her father was dozing. There was only one thing she wanted to remember about this day: she just wanted to recall that the sun was out, and that last night's tempest had blown pretty shells onto the beach.

◦~◦

Chief Constable Holt pushed his chair back and lit his cigar.

"I'd say that about does it, gents," he said, drawing a satisfied puff.

"I'm afraid so," frowned Inspector Downes, a smartly clad man in his thirties. "It's a shame, really."

"A shame?" Dr. McCabe wondered.

"Yes, this was the first case in which I was wrong," the younger man complained, twiddling with a pencil. "But I had some reason to draw the conclusions I did, as I'm sure you both agree. By all the accounts I gathered in the village, this Mrs. Abernathy was the most devoted of nurses. I had no cause to suspect she would injure her patient. And anyway, I never found any evidence to suggest she was responsible."

"Ah, but you wouldn't have," Holt interrupted. "Abernathy—or the commandant, really—would have taken care of that. We learned he was seen in that neighborhood shortly before Starbuck's daughter returned. Like as not, he found his lady dead, swiped the incriminating evidence, and then just quietly made his own plans for revenge on the man who killed his wife."

"Provided Starbuck killed her," interjected the doctor.

"I said *killed*, not murdered, McCabe," Holt replied irritably. "Let's not go over that again."

"I know what you said, Halsted. But who is to say that's how it happened? For instance, we have assumed this Mrs. Abernathy was as insane as her husband and personally set about to destroy Starbuck. But mightn't we be wrong? Everyone commented on how sincere she appeared in her devotion to Starbuck. Perhaps the woman really cared about her patient and was merely terrified into her role by her husband. You'll recall the police surgeon found several bruises on her; these he attributed to Starbuck, but it might have been otherwise.

"Abernathy may have injured Starbuck himself. Starbuck might have pulled himself free of those ropes that tied him to the chair and escaped. Then Abernathy could have gone after him and been stopped by his wife. In truth, we really don't know if Starbuck committed the deed or if Abernathy did it in his rage."

"If you look at it that way, then no one will ever know what happened," Downes snorted.

"God knows," the doctor replied. "And if you think about it from the standpoint of justice, He's really the only One Who needs to."

It was warm. That was what was so strange about it. It had always been cold. Every day it was cold; every night it was frigid. But now it was warm. And then there was the noise: there was none. Well, there was, but it was a resonant, reassuring sort of noise. No one was screaming and no one was shouting. There was no rattle of machine gun fire or sharp report of pistols.

Something was wrong.

He opened his eyes, and instantly the world became blinding white. Blinking painfully, he held up his hand and looked downward.

There was no snow on the ground. Instead, it was covered in pebbles and shale and *sand* of all things. Reaching down, he picked up a stone and felt the warmth of it soak into his hand.

Thhhhooommm...Thhhooommm, went the soothing boom around him.

He looked up.

It was ocean. It was real ocean. He could not believe it.

Staggering to his feet, he stumbled forward into the lapping froth of the tide and stood up to his ankles in rich, rolling saltwater. It was so beautiful. It was unspeakably delicious. The only thing better than standing here in the dying waves would be to ride on the waves themselves.

Perhaps there was a boat nearby?

For the first time, he started really looking around him, down the beach to the pier, behind him at the white cliffs. It all was so glorious and fresh that he hardly knew what to do with the overwhelming sense of life inside him.

But soon he saw something that made him feel more than alive. Further up the beach was the figure of a child bending down and puttering with something in the sand. The breeze was whipping her pastel pink skirt about her snowy knees and making her auburn hair flash in the sunlight.

She was beautiful, even more beautiful than the warm stone and the sound of the waves and the feeling of the ocean against his ankles. Presently, she turned, saw him, and started walking his way.

For a moment, he was afraid. And then he was terrified. He was terrified because he was so unaccountably content. No, not content. It was some other feeling.

He was happy. He was happy, but it was as if he were happy for the first time. And he had no idea what to do about it.

"Daddy, be careful. Don't go too far out," the child said, walking over and taking his hand to bring him back.

Her hand was so soft and small. He looked down at it and then up at her face. Now he knew what to do.

Without warning, Ulysses grabbed her in a crushing embrace. It was so unexpected that the poor girl shrieked in fear and squirmed.

"Daddy, stop!" she squeaked. "Aunty, Uncle Morton, somebody help!"

Ulysses was too weak from his recent misfortunes to hold her long. As soon as he let go, the child darted for the cliff path. Yet after several paces, she stopped and turned around, looking at that expression of dumfounded delight on his face.

"Daddy?" she called, stepping cautiously in his direction.

She was coming back. That was all he understood. When she got close enough, he tried hugging her again.

This time she hugged him back.

"Daddy, please say something," she spoke.

But he didn't know how to respond. He felt as though something were missing, that he was supposed to know something and did not. But what it was he could not guess.

"Daddy," said the girl, "it's Eva."

In an instant, the fog cleared, the spell was broken, and the daylight rushed in as through a window rapidly un-curtained. The sheer number of memories that flooded into his consciousness was so overwhelming that it was all he could do to stay standing.

And then the grief came, and it brought him to his knees.

"Dear God," he breathed. "Oh, God help me!"

"Daddy, you're talking!" Eva cried excitedly. "Daddy, you're *talking*!"

"Eva," he rasped.

"I'm here, Daddy!" the girl replied, hugging him again and kissing his face. "I'm here, I'm here!"

"Sweetheart, I'm so sorry!" he said, his voice breaking.

"Don't cry, Daddy!" the child gasped. "What's wrong? Please don't cry!"

"I—I promised. Sweetheart, how old are you?"

"Thirteen!"

That was too much for him, and he began weeping irrepressibly.

"Please stop," Eva said, crying herself. "Please don't cry anymore!"

"Seven years!"

"I know, but it wasn't your fault. It's all right now. You're back! Please stop crying."

He did not stop for a long time. And all the while, Eva patted

229

him and kissed him as though he were the child and not her. But eventually, he forced himself to his feet and stood there in the sunlight, gazing at the new world around him and holding on to his daughter's hand.

For a moment, they were silent, with the calm, cool sea water tugging playfully at their feet.

"Eva," he said at length, "I feel so lost. It's been so dark."

"It's all right, Daddy."

"But I don't know how I got home. I don't know how long I've been back or what I've done here. I don't—I don't know myself anymore. I feel hollowed out. I feel like I've been dead!"

"Daddy, you're shaking," Eva said, squeezing his trembling hand with both of hers. "It's going to be all right. It will get better."

"Eva?"

"Yes, Daddy?"

"I love you, Eva," her father whispered. "Wherever I've been, whatever I've done, I have always loved you."

The child rested her head on his arm and smiled.

"I know, Daddy," she said. "And I love you, too."

"When I fall, I shall arise; when I sit in darkness, the Lord shall be a light unto me.... He will bring me forth to the light."
Micah 7:8b, 9b KJV

Lightning Source UK Ltd.
Milton Keynes UK
UKHW041515020921
389715UK00020B/495/J

9 781664 238817